Grain of Wheat

MICHAEL EDWARD GIESLER

GRAIN OF WHEAT

 Scepter

Scripture texts on pages 21 and 167 (as indicated) are taken from the Holy Bible, Revised Standard Version, Catholic Edition, © 1965 and 1966 by the Division of Christian Education of the National Council of the Churches of Christ in the United States. All rights reserved. Used with permission.

All other Scripture quotation used in this book are taken from the Confraternity Edition of the Bible.

Previous volumes in the trilogy:
  Junia (2002)
  Marcus (2004)

Grain of Wheat
© 2008 Michael Edward Giesler

Published by Scepter Publishers, Inc.
www.scepterpublishers.org
All rights reserved

ISBN 978-1-59417-078-2

FIRST PRINTING 2008

Text composed in Adobe Caslon fonts

Printed in the United States of America

*Dedicated
to the Christian faithful of Rome
living in the second century of our era,
most of whom are anonymous,
but whose example and dedication to Christ
helped to transform the pagan world*

Note to the Reader

The historical characters in this book include: persons named in the New Testament, Saint Justin Martyr, Pope Pius I, the Emperor Antoninus, and the Gnostics Valentinus and Marcion. The others are fictional. The footnotes provide historical and scriptural background.

MAIN CHARACTERS FROM THE FIRST TWO BOOKS

JUNIA—daughter of Gaius Metellus Cimber, wealthy Senator of Rome. She is killed in the Colosseum for the crime of being a Christian.

MARCUS—philosopher brother of Junia, who becomes a Christian three years after Junia's death.

AURELIA—wife of Gaius Metellus Cimber, and mother of Marcus and Junia.

MARCIA—Junia's best friend, who is killed with her father Diodorus of Corinth for the crime of being Christians.

CYNTHIA—personal servant of Junia, who later becomes a Christian.

SCINTILLA—kitchen slave in Marcia's household, who instructs first Junia, then Cynthia in Christianity.

DÉDICUS—philosophy student from Samaria who saves Marcus's life.

NUMER—Egyptian friend of Dédicus, who instructs Marcus in the principles of Christian belief.

ATTICUS—young priest from Gaul, who teaches Marcus about the life of Christ.

LIVIA—daughter of Antonius and Agrippina, who spy on Junia and denounce her as a Christian.

SERVIANUS (Servi)—brother of Livia, and boyhood friend of Marcus.

JUSTUS—fish merchant who lives outside of Rome, and is married to Constantia (Consti). Their children are Timotheus (Timo) and Carmina.

DISCALUS—fish-shop owner in Rome and friend of Justus; he married Silvia, after his first wife died.

GAIUS—only son of Discalus, and best friend of Timotheus.

TITUS—student of law from a noble family; friend of Numer and Dédicus.

QUINTUS—head of the Praetorian Guard, and former suitor of Junia.

CLAUDIA—wife of Quintus, and former mistress of Cynthia, after Junia died.

BOMBOLINUS (Bombo)—political assistant of Senator Gaius Metellus Cimber.

Contents

PRELUDE

I.

Marcus looked at Italy's shore from the large grain and passenger ship. They were approaching Puteoli, from where he had embarked just a year before with Numer and Dédicus, who had saved him from the racing chariot just after Junia's death. He had learned much in Alexandria, especially about refuting the errors of the Gnostics. He had even composed a tract against Basilides for his portrayal of Christ as a kind of *aeon*, or subordinate god to the one Divine Being.

But it was time to return; he had promised his father that he would be abroad only for a year. His mother Aurelia had been writing to him once a month with news about the house on the Esquiline, and trying to convince him each time to abandon Christianity. "It's so dangerous, Marcus," she had put in her last letter, "and based on a superstition. Please reconsider your decision, for your father's sake. I have said nothing to him, as I promised. But at times I think he suspects something; please don't make the same mistake as your sister did. I love you." Those words had wrenched him to his heart's core, but they did not surprise him. He felt that his commitment to Jesus the Christ had become stronger than ever before, but it would be very hard for him to face his parents now . . . his mother with her tears, his father with his outraged shock and disappointment.

He might even be disowned, like his sister.

He consoled himself by considering that at least he had one less burden to face; Aurelia had written that Antonius, Livia's father, had died suddenly. It was Antonius's plot against him, to denounce him as a Christian, which had prompted him to leave the city so suddenly the year before. He felt that now he had some chance to work for Christ in Rome, though for how long he did not know. He had also heard that Hadrian had died at his sumptuous villa near Tivoli, and that Antoninus was now Emperor. Marcus did not know much about him, but had heard from friends in Alexandria that he had no particular desire to persecute Christians; he would continue the policy of Trajan and Hadrian, namely that Christians could be prosecuted only if there was a clear accusation from a personal witness, followed by a fair trial. Anonymous denunciations would not be accepted.

The large Roman vessel, with its broad sail loosened and two hundred people aboard, was now approaching the dock. Marcus said a prayer to his protecting spirit, who had taken such good care of him the previous year in Egypt, with its exotic dangers and temptations. But his angel would have to work much harder for him now on the treacherous streets of Rome.

RETURN TO ROME

II.

Aurelia had sent a *raeda*[1] driven by Syphon to the port at Puteoli. As Marcus walked down the large wooden plank of the ship, he waved to the slave who had played games with him when he was a boy. He had not changed much: perhaps an extra gray hair or two, but with the same cool and self-possessed manner. But now Marcus knew that he had a different relationship with him. During their long journey to Rome on the Via Appia, along the coast of the sea, he prayed that someday he would be able to bring him to the Christ.

When they reached Rome, whose streets Marcus knew so well, he asked Syphon to take his large traveling bag home, and to let him off so that he could walk on the streets of the city once again, which he loved to do.

"Master Marcus," the slave responded with the confidence of an old friend, "your mother requests that you be driven all the way home today."

At that Marcus smiled, and obediently remained in the back seat of the *raeda* until they reached the white stone columns of his father's mansion on the Esquiline Hill. His mother was at the door, waiting for him. She was wearing a light blue tunic with a silver brooch at her neck. As he climbed the steps she opened her arms to receive him; there were tears in her eyes.

It was clear to Marcus that she still loved him, despite his religion, which in her eyes was so perverse.

"Oh, Marcus, Marcus, *vale! Vale!* I have missed you so!"

---

[1] Passenger carriage or wagon with four wheels, drawn by one to four horses.

Marcus kissed her tenderly and softly touched her light blonde hair. "And I've missed you also, *mater carissima*, and thank you so much for your letters every month. You look to be in good health."

"I am, my son. And you—you have the dark face of an Egyptian!"

"Yes, it's from all the sun in that land, I'm sure. It will probably wear off in a month or so. But tell me, is Father well?"

"He's at the Emperor's country villa for a few days."

"Really?" Marcus said with some surprise. "But he's no longer Consul. Why would the Emperor want to see him?"

"Antoninus was always impressed with your father's oratorical skills. He needs him to speak to the Senate about his new program for Rome."

"And what is that?"

"To save millions of sesterces this year; he wants to put Rome back in good financial order."

"I wish him luck in that one," Marcus laughed. "I've never heard of an Emperor who's been able to save money."

As they entered the atrium, in front of the large red and white mosaic of the goddess Minerva, Aurelia turned to him suddenly, with a serious, almost somber look on her face.

"Did you receive my last letter, Marcus? About your being a Christian?"

Marcus would have preferred to avoid that topic, and simply speak to her about the sights of Egypt, but he could see it was very much on her mind. He said a prayer to the Holy Spirit; he would not deceive her.

"Yes I did, Mother. Please try to understand. It's a deep commitment of my mind, and my heart. I cannot change it; to follow the Christ means everything for me. I love you and Father even more now, as a Christian. Please believe me."

With those words Aurelia's face looked even more concerned, and Marcus saw lines of worry on her forehead that he had never seen before.

"Your father will be enraged, Marcus. He may even dis-own you."

"Dear Mother," he said as he gently stroked her cheek with his right hand, "I'm prepared to take that risk."

III.

Marcus was glad for the chance to wait a few days before breaking the news to his father about his religion. It would give him a chance to speak with Atticus, who along with Numer had brought him to the Way. They arranged to meet in front of the Aventine House, where Titus and some of his friends still lived. After his ordination, Atticus had moved from the house and was now living with a priest from Antioch, where the Apostle Paul had first spread Christ's word almost a hundred years earlier. But the young priest enjoyed being with his friends at the Aventine and kept seeing them: like himself they had given up everything for the sake of the Lord Christ, though they were not ordained.[2]

As he walked toward that familiar hill again, he passed by the Colosseum where he could hear a huge crowd roaring inside. *Who's being killed today?* Marcus asked himself with some bitterness. It was probably a gladiatorial match, since he had not heard of any Christian who had been denounced or condemned. He said a short prayer for the men being killed, and another one for their killers. *Somehow, someday,* he thought to himself, *the Savior will win this city to his love.*

He found Atticus waiting for him at the courtyard in front of the house, where they had often spoken before. They embraced each other Roman style, and Marcus could feel strength in the young priest's arms. He looked confi-dently into Atticus's dark blue eyes; there was a wrinkle or

---

[2] The practice of celibacy was highly esteemed in the first centuries of the Church, as a way of imitating more closely the life of Christ and his apostles, and of spreading his kingdom. It was not restricted to priests.

two already on his young face, but his lips were smiling broadly as they had always done before.

"*Vale*, Marcus, you look even smarter!"

"I wish it were so, Atticus. I did get a lot of training in Alexandria, especially for unmasking Basilides's errors, and those of his Gnostic friends . . . but I have a lot to learn."

"Yes, I can imagine, and it won't be long before some of those errors get to Rome. It's good that you are back, Marcus; we need you. But tell me, how are Numer and Dédicus?"

"They're both in good health, though I can still outwrestle them."

"Even Numer?"

"Even Numer; he's fast, but he still doesn't know all the tricks. Both of them are staying at a small house near the sea that a Christian family in Alexandria loaned to them. Two or three other disciples have joined them, who have a similar interest in philosophy."

"So they continue to do what they did in Rome," said Atticus. "It's the mustard seed that Our Lord described. But tell me, Marcus, how are your father and mother? Did you ever tell them you were a Christian?"

"My mother knows. I told her before I went to Egypt. She took it very hard, and is now especially worried about what my father will do when he hears it."

"It looks like we'll have to pray a lot," the young priest from Gaul answered. "But I have a few ideas that may help you with your parents; I've been thinking about it since I heard that you were returning."

Then both of them sat down on the marble bench next to the rectangular pool, and spoke for almost two hours.

IV.

Gaius returned from the Emperor's villa in Lorium in a buoyant mood. During the twelve mile journey, he could not help feeling privileged, though he tried not to become emotional about it, since he was a practicing Stoic. Emperor Antoninus obviously had a great deal of trust in him, after observing him carefully for some time. Despite his daughter's execution as a Christian, Gaius had handled the consulship well under the last years of Hadrian, particularly in his dealings with the Senate. The Emperor gave him to understand that he would be relying on him especially to promote his fiscal program for Rome in the years ahead.

Gaius found Marcus waiting for him in his study, next to the atrium; it was about the seventh hour of the day, when many Romans went to the baths. Marcus was dressed in a clean white tunic, and had carefully trimmed his light brown beard. As his father entered, he ran up to him and embraced him.

"Marcus, my son," Gaius said, withdrawing from him a bit so as not to appear too emotional, "how good it is to see you again. It's been over a year."

"I've missed you, Father," Marcus answered sincerely, though in his heart he was trembling about what he had to tell him.

"The Emperor has been very good to me, Marcus; I will be one of his personal advisors for the foreseeable future," Gaius began, trying to muffle the little tone of pride in his voice.

"It is as I thought, Father. Antoninus recognizes your accomplishments, and obviously needs you for his economic program," Marcus replied, without hiding the fact that he was proud of his father.

Gaius looked carefully at his son's face. The same inquisitive eyes, the same resolute jaw, though his face was considerably darker because of the Egyptian sun. "And you, my son, what are your plans now in Rome?"

"I made some excellent contacts in Alexandria, and I've returned with a recommendation from Demetrion, one of the most famous Platonists there, for a teaching position at the Athenaeum. I think I can get it easily."

"Good," Gaius responded. Long ago he had given up the battle to convince him to go into politics. "And how old are you now?"

"Twenty-six, Father."

"Twenty-six, and still not married. For the sake of the family name, to propagate the great heritage of Metellus Cimber, I would like you to marry as soon as possible, Marcus. I have already chosen an excellent woman for you—Elvira, daughter of Senator Tullius. The family is very well connected, and I want you to meet her."

Marcus ground his teeth together nervously, and shifted his weight from one foot to the other. He was hoping that his father would not bring up the marriage question so soon. He said a brief prayer to the Holy Spirit, as Atticus had urged him to do, and answered in a low but confident voice: "Father, I have something very important to tell you."

"Yes," Gaius answered, with a look of vague apprehension in his eyes.

"Could we go out to the courtyard, and sit down? I think this will take a bit of time."

Gaius, though a busy man, had reserved the remaining hours of the afternoon for his son, and accompanied him to the peristylium; they both sat on the marble bench there next to the fountain, where Junia used to sit and read.

"Do you recall, Father, that five years ago I was saved from being run over by a wild charioteer in the street? It was a young fellow from Samaria who saved me."

"Yes, I do remember. One of the strangest things I had ever heard of . . . but then the people from that part of the world are quite strange. Nevertheless, of course, I am very grateful to him," Gaius answered emphatically.

"As you recall we came to know each other quite well; he too was interested in philosophy. His Latin name is Dédicus, and he introduced me to a group of his friends who lived in a house on the Aventine Hill."

"Yes, I remember," Gaius answered. Somewhere he had

heard that that house had a connection with the Christians, but had suppressed it from his mind. He had too many other things to occupy him at the time.

"Father, Dédicus and those men truly changed my life for the good. Not only did I learn a new and exciting philosophical system from them, especially regarding the Logos, but I found a whole new way of living. In some ways it is like Stoicism, since it teaches virtue and self-control, but it goes beyond that to speak of a God who is a true redeemer and cares for every human being."

"A god who is a redeemer? The Stoics would never go that far."

"I know that, Father. But that is precisely what fascinated me. As a matter of fact, I became so interested in this new way of thinking and living that I have dedicated my life to it."

"Is that so? Is it one of those Eastern mystery religions, like the new Platonic movement, or the cult of Mithra?"

Marcus halted for a moment. "It's much more than those, Father; it's far more demanding, and . . ."—here his voice began to waver as he looked away from his father—"and it's far more dangerous."

For the first time Gaius looked at his son with a trace of fear in his eyes. For a moment he looked down at the finely hewn stonework at their feet, as if trying to escape from something that he knew he had to face. But then he asked slowly, very deliberately: "And what is this religion, my son? Tell me clearly."

"Father, I am a Christian."

Gaius put the back of his right hand to his forehead. At first he experienced a deep confusion that made him feel dizzy; then very suddenly, he experienced a strong surge of anger welling up within him, the same feeling as when Junia had told him that she was a Christian four years earlier.

He abruptly stood up from the marble bench, and looked down severely at his son.

"Do you realize that Christianity is a capital crime against the Roman state, punishable by death?"

"I know, Father," Marcus answered almost inaudibly.

Raising his voice more, Gaius went on.

"And do you know that it is an irrational superstition, based on the belief of a man rising from the dead who was crucified by a Roman governor for treason?"

"It's not a superstition, Father. It's a true belief based on eyewitness reports, and on many miracles that this man performed before and even after his death."

"No, my son," Gaius answered firmly. "It is a cult that is subverting the Roman Empire, and drawing people away from giving honor to Caesar."

Atticus had advised Marcus not to argue with his father, but he felt obliged to answer him. "Father, all the Christians that I know are hardworking honest citizens of the Empire, though many of them are slaves. They have good families, they don't drink or carouse with women, and they pay their taxes. They're truly supporting Caesar, not undermining him."

"Then why don't they offer incense to his statue, as people of other religions do across the Empire? They're in clear disobedience to the law, and in their fanaticism they refuse to listen to reason."

"But, Father, try to understand. They're not dishonoring Caesar; they're honoring the God they believe in. Their faith means so much to them that they are willing . . ."

But Gaius cut him off. "Faith? What is faith? I taught you knowledge and common sense for so many years in this house, but now you're inventing strange words, and want me to agree with you. Listen Marcus," he said looking directly into his eyes, "I will not allow a Christian to live in my house. You are jeopardizing both your mother and me, and putting me at great personal risk with the Emperor. If you do not renounce your superstition, you must leave this house tomorrow morning."

"But, Father, I would like to speak more about this with you and explain my belief. It will take time."

"You have said enough. Tell your mother goodbye or whatever you wish, but I will not harbor an enemy of Caesar in my home."

Then he turned away quickly and walked into his study. As Marcus rose from the bench and was about to return to his room, he saw his mother standing at the entrance of his sister's old room. She had obviously been listening to the whole conversation. Her body was trembling, and there were tears in her eyes. Marcus went to her and embraced her; she let herself be held at first, but then she pushed him away. "I told you so, Marcus, I told you so," she cried out, running from the room.

V.

From the days of his catechumenate Marcus had heard the Master's prediction that "son shall go against father, and father against son, and mother against daughter . . ."[3] Knowing that prediction in some way lessened the pain of what had just happened to him, but it could not take it away. He felt his hands shaking and tears coming to his eyes as he left Junia's old room to go to his own. Now he knew what she had had to go through.

At least, he thought to himself, his father had not disowned him . . . not yet.

He did have many friends in the city. He thought at first of going to the house on the Aventine: there he had met Numer and Atticus, there he had learned of Christ for the first time, there he had actually seen Christ in the words and

---

[3] The exact Gospel text says: "Do not think that I have come to bring peace on earth; I have not come to bring peace, but a sword. For I have come to set a man against his father, and a daughter against her mother, and a daughter-in-law against mother-in-law. . . . He who loves father or mother more than me is not worthy of me" (Mt 10: 34–35, 37); RSV–CE.

actions of the young men who lived there. But he did not want to expose them to danger. To live at that house—he the son of Gaius, former Consul of Rome and now personal confidant of the Emperor—would attract far too much attention. His friends could all be denounced as Christians. So he decided to rent a small flat near the Athenaeum, if he could find the money. From there he could walk easily to the school, where he would try to work and support himself as a teacher. The recommendation that he had from Demetrion, one of the foremost Platonists in Alexandria, would be almost a sure entry for some kind of position.

As Marcus was packing his bag the next day, he heard footsteps at the entrance of his room: it was his mother. She had composed herself from yesterday's tempest, and actually entered his room with a little smile on her face. She had a leather bag in her hand.

"Your father and I want you to have this, Marcus."

Marcus shook the bag and heard the sound of coins inside.

"It's five hundred sesterces. That should be enough to pay the rent for a house in the city until you can find some income."

Marcus looked inquisitively at his mother, not knowing what to say. He shook his head slowly and answered, "You didn't have to do this for me, Mother. I know how you and father feel . . ."

But Aurelia went up to him and kissed him. "You will always be our son, Marcus. But please, please be careful. It would destroy us both if you ended up like your sister."

VI.

The son of Gaius and Aurelia obtained a lecturing post at the Athenaeum right away, so he really didn't need the money. He had already made a good name for himself in his previous years there, and now, with the recommendation of

Demetrion and his experience in Alexandria, his position was assured. He had also perfected his knowledge of Greek abroad; he could speak it almost without accent. He had analyzed all of Plato's dialogues, and could comment on them in their original language. He also had the joy of seeing Servianus again, Livia's brother, who was teaching Aristotle's works at the Athenaeum.

The day after getting the appointment, Servianus and he went horseback riding in a large wooded field outside the city. They found the same log where they had sat a year before, and Servianus had warned Marcus of his father's plot against him.

"I'm sorry about the sudden death of your father, Servianus."

The young man looked at him incredulously. "Can you really mean that, Marcus? After all that he did to you and your family?"

"I do mean it. As a matter of fact, when I first heard of his sudden death in Egypt, I said a prayer to the Christian God for him."

Servianus looked back at him at first in surprise, but then with a knowing smile on his slim face he said: "What an amazing cult you belong to, Marcus. But then you're only trying to follow what Jesus Christ said, aren't you? To love your enemies as yourself?"

"Where did you learn that, Servianus?"

"Are you ready for a little surprise?"

"Yes," Marcus answered a bit nervously, as he leaned forward on the log. He had had many surprises in his life, and some of them had not been pleasant. The sun was about to set, casting long shadows upon them through the trees.

"I'm speaking with Father Nicanor, a presbyter from Cyprus, about Christianity. His last talk with me was on the virtue of charity."

Marcus was speechless, as he felt his heart skip a beat.

He had been praying for his friend during the year in Egypt, but he never dreamt that in such a short time the son of his greatest enemy would be thinking seriously about the Church. He turned to his friend, and gave him a big embrace.

"Whoa, Marcus," Servianus said jokingly, "I am not there yet. . . . I still have many questions. And it's not the safest religion in the world, you know."

THE FAMILY OF CHRIST

VII.

Cynthia, now a freed woman, was worried about Scintilla. She was staying in a small tenement apartment near the old forum, and her health was failing quickly. After Diodorus and Marcia were killed, she had worked as a kitchen servant in the household of Marius, who was a Christian; after a few years he had granted her freedom. Cynthia knew that Scintilla could never retire from serving her real Master, and that she would continue to help others tirelessly to discover the Christ even in her old age. She considered the time to be very short before he would return again, as some other disciples did, and frequently prayed the *Maranatha*[4] invocation.

Two slaves, Statira from Syria and Frieda from Germany, came often to visit and take care of her, preparing meals if she was too weak to prepare her own. Both of them worked in Marius's household, and both were Christians who had learned the Way from Scintilla.

Cynthia also visited her once a week, and more if needed. One afternoon Scintilla was dozing at her chair near the window, so Cynthia silently walked up to her and sat down on the floor next to her. She thought of all that Scintilla had done for so many people in Rome over the previous thirty years, from her conversion during Trajan's reign, shortly after Bishop Ignatius's death in the Colosseum. She had first met her when she delivered Marcia's letter to Junia, and afterward she recalled how jealous she felt at the long hours that

[4] An ancient prayer that begins with the Aramaic word meaning *Come, Lord*, referring particularly to the *parousia* or second coming of Christ to the world.

Scintilla would spend with Junia teaching her about the Lord Christ, while Cynthia and everyone else thought she was teaching her Gallic language and customs only!

She would never forget that day at the Vatican Hill cemetery just after her father's funeral, when she saw Scintilla with a group of Christians praying at Peter's resting place. She had thought it so strange that people would be praying for a man named PETROS.[5] Though she had kept her distance, Scintilla had recognized her, went up to her and embraced her. It was such a depressing time in her life, and she had felt so alone . . . it was Scintilla that gave her hope again, and afterward even more hope and love when she began to teach her about the Christ. How could she ever pay her back, this wonderful person from Gaul who didn't even know Greek? She stood up and walked to Scintilla's chair quietly; then she kissed her lightly on the forehead, which woke her up.

The older woman opened her eyes suddenly and saw Cynthia, who was dressed in a light pink tunic, and as was her custom, with a small white chrysanthemum in her hair. She shook her head as if reprimanding herself. "Here I am dozing away, Cynthia, when there are so many people I should be seeing. But I can't do much anymore," she said, almost sadly.

"Oh, Scintilla," the Greek girl said as she took her hand, "don't worry. You're doing much more just sitting here and praying for us all. Don't you remember what you taught me about the power of prayer to the Lord *Kúrios*?"

Scintilla smiled. Cynthia loved to use that Greek word for the Lord all the time, while most of the other Christians in Rome would say *Dominus*.

"Tell me," Cynthia continued as she stroked the woman's matted gray hair gently, smoothing out the rough spots. "Have you been praying for my student Portia? She's someone that I'd like to bring to you soon. She's one of my best

[5] The Greek name for Peter, meaning "rock."

students, and I've begun to tell her about the Way as I teach her Greek."

"That's what I did for Junia, except it was Gallic," Scintilla said softly with a little laugh under her breath.

"Yes," Cynthia's dark eyes lit up as she nodded. "She's the daughter of Lentullus, an equestrian who lives near the Via Sacra. She's not even fifteen, but she has a good mind for practical things, and most of all, she really cares for people. She keeps asking when she can meet some real Christians, instead of just hearing about them. She's not afraid."

"I would love to meet her," Scintilla answered in a low voice, but then she coughed and looked away. Cynthia saw a little trickle of blood coming from the side of her mouth.

VIII.

The next day Cynthia brought Portia to meet Scintilla. It was just after sunrise, when Scintilla had completed her morning prayer to the Lord Christ. Statira and Frieda were preparing breakfast for her, a warm chicken broth with figs and freshly baked bread. Scintilla looked carefully at Cynthia's student: a pretty girl of medium height with brown hair, wearing a light blue tunic and black sandals. The girl smiled eagerly when she saw Scintilla, and bowed deeply to her.

"Oh, no, you don't have to do that, little one!" the elderly freedwoman protested with an embarrassed grin on her face. "I'm not so venerable; you'll spoil me."

Portia's light brown eyes lit up, as she raised her eyebrows. "But you *are* special, lady Scintilla, because you brought both Junia and Cynthia to the Lord Christ. I am just now learning about him . . ."

"It was the Holy Spirit that brought them, not I, Portia. But you have a very good teacher in Cynthia; I hope you're paying attention."

"I think I'm learning about Christianity faster than

Greek. Sometimes I get my Greek conjugations confused, but Cynthia says that my pronunciation is pretty good."

Cynthia tapped her lightly on the shoulder. "That's true, daughter of Lentullus, but you still have that Latin accent; Junia had it also, especially when she tried to say the word *pneuma*." [6] Portia laughed, and Cynthia squeezed her hand affectionately. Then turning to Scintilla, she sat on the floor in front of her, with Portia at her side, and she motioned to the others to do the same.

"Why don't you tell us a few things about the first times, Scintilla? Who did you know when you joined the Way? Did you ever speak with anyone who had met the Master himself, or one of his apostles?"

"I actually met the Way through a Syrian girl—like you, Statira—who brought me to the first gathering shortly after Ignatius died in the Colosseum. I was tremendously moved by that old man's calm and courage, as the beasts attacked him. After that, the little Syrian introduced to me to Eunice, who was nearly fifty years old then. She was from a little town near Ephesus, and she remembers as a girl meeting Mary of Magdala herself."

"The Magadalene herself! What a privilege!" they all shouted at once.

"Yes," Scintilla answered nodding slowly, "the very one who personally served the Master and his apostles, and who first saw him raised from the tomb. Eunice knew her in her final days, but she was alert and speaking with people until the end."

"What was she like?"

"She was tall with dark eyes that looked right through you," Eunice told me, "but you always had the impression that she loved you at the same time . . ."

"Perhaps like the Master's glance . . ." Cynthia offered.

"Yes, I think so," Scintilla continued. "She spoke often of how wonderful it was for her and the others to serve the

[6] The Greek word for spirit.

Master and his apostles during those days in Galilee and Judaea. She must have seen his glance many times. They would travel in big groups, but the men always slept in a separate area from the women. The women, especially Mary of Magdala, Salomé the mother of James and John, and Mary of Clopas, were in charge of preparing the meals for the Master and his apostles. They would also wash their clothing, including their robes, when they were traveling."

"I would love to see Jesus' robe," Portia burst out enthusiastically.

"Yes," Cynthia added, "the one that his mother wove for him. The women of Galilee are the best linen makers in the world."

"I heard that the Roman soldiers cast lots for it," Frieda said with her thick Germanic accent, "how lucky the soldier who won it."

"True," Scintilla answered, "and I'm sure that Mary Magdalene and the others washed that robe many times in the rivers and wells of Palestine; they must have patched up some holes in it too, since Jesus walked so much and had so many people around him all the time."

"I wish I could have seen Mary Magdalene," Statira said regretfully. "But alas, I was born too late."

"Don't be concerned, Statira," Scintilla answered as she turned away and coughed a little bit. After taking a deep breath, she said: "We are continuing her work, teaching others the Faith as she did, and serving the Lord's apostles."

"Is that why you and Eunice began to cook meals for Bishop Telesphorus and some of the other presbyters in the city?"

"Yes," the elderly woman from Gaul answered. "We clean for them also. That was one of the things that Mary Magdalene and the others learned from the Mother of Jesus after he died. She continued serving her Son by helping his apostles. She herself insisted on serving John's family after he took her into his home, but many times they would not let her do it."

"You mean, after the crucifixion?"

"Yes, she was so humble that she never wanted any praise or honor, but people kept offering it to her, and going to her for help and prayers. She just wanted to serve people, as her Son did."

"Of all the Mary's, she's the one I would most love to meet, though I'll have to wait for His Coming. In the meantime I pray to her every day," Frieda said.

"She's the one who said *Behold the handmaid of the Lord . . .*—right, Cynthia?" Portia asked.

"You've got that one right, little one," Scintilla answered, as she beckoned her to stand up and come to her. She kissed the young woman on her forehead and said, "She's not only the Mother of Jesus, she's the Mother of all of us."

Portia looked rather perplexed after hearing that; but then she thought about it a little, and smiled. After that, they all laughed.

IX.

Marcus began lecturing at the beginning of the eighth month of the year, which the Romans called October. There were students from around the Empire: Spain, North Africa, Asia, even parts of Gaul and Germany. He soon established himself as a brilliant lecturer and debater: not only was he a native Roman who had studied at the Athenaeum for five years, but also he had worked in Alexandria and met some of the greatest Platonists there. Numer loaned him his uncle's manuscripts, which had been saved from the previous library in Alexandria that had been destroyed by fire two hundred years earlier. Marcus could read and comment upon the most controversial dialogues, especially the *Phaedo* and the *Republic.* He had also composed a refutation of the Gnostic Basilides, with his endless genealogies of subordinate beings

flowing from the One, but he had written it on purely schol-
arly terms, since he wanted no one to suspect that he was a
Christian.

One day a week Marcus and Servianus would have supper
together. Marcus had become a decent cook in Egypt, and
Servianus joked that all of Marcus's meals had a certain
"Egyptian" flavor to them, which the latter took to be a
compliment, but was not certain about it. After supper they
would speak mostly of philosophical matters, when Marcus
would try to answer his friend's questions about Christianity.
Another day of the week they would have a meal with the
fellows on the Aventine Hill, and joined their gathering
afterward.

Titus had become the leader of the group after Numer
left for Egypt. He didn't have Numer's fun-loving spirit or
athletic prowess, but he was very intelligent and the other
fellows respected him. More recently he had become quite
absorbed in his effort to be named a quaestor.[7] Marcus admired Titus's ambition, but he knew that he was playing a
very dangerous game because he was a Christian. What's
more, he had to please certain minor officials to get his name
recognized for office, and some of them were known to be
unscrupulous. As a result Titus often seemed to be moody
and tense about things.

"Titus," Marcus asked him one day as they were leaving
the dining room and entering the atrium, where Marcus had
first met him several years before, "is there anything troubling you?"

"Oh, nothing," Titus answered with a little hesitation in
his voice.

"There must be something. Does it have to do with the
quaestorship?"

"Yes, it does," his friend answered, but said nothing more.
Marcus noted that he didn't want to talk anymore about it,

---

[7] An appointed official of the Roman government in charge of finances. This
office was also considered to be the first step towards a seat in the Senate.

so he said a brief prayer to his angel for him. Titus was the one who had brought Dédicus to the Church, and of course Dédicus had brought him. He would always remember the original poem that Titus had read for Atticus during his first visit to the Aventine, and the encouraging way he had greeted him on the street when he was still a catechumen. He said a prayer for him, knowing that he must be under a lot of pressure.

X.

As they had done often before, Marcus and Servianus went horseback riding in a field beyond the Via Flaminia. "It must have been hard for you when your father died," the son of Gaius said, as they approached a more wooded area. Servianus looked at him appreciatively, remembering how Marcus had asked about his father before. But such a thoughtful comment is what it meant to be a Christian, he reflected. "Not really hard, Marcus. I was never close to him; he always seemed more interested in the Senate than he was in his family."

"And how are your mother and sister Livia doing?"

"After the mourning period, Mother plans to remarry. She already has someone in mind, a wealthy olive merchant who lives near the Capitoline. He just divorced his first wife."

Marcus said nothing; he was not surprised, since divorce was very common in Rome. But it was against the Master's teaching.

"And Livia?"

"She is quite unhappy, and continuously talks about divorce, though she still lives at her husband's estate near Capua." [8]

"Was she ever able to have a child?"

"That's part of the tragedy of it, Marcus. Livia wants one very badly, but her husband thinks it would be an intolerable

[8] Capua was the capital city of Campania, a district of Central Italy.

burden which would interfere with their lifestyle. It's also widely rumored that he has had affairs with two married women in Rome."

"Poor Livia," Marcus said, though he could not banish the thought that she was suffering for having betrayed his sister. But he resolved to keep praying for her.

XI.

Aurelia was concerned about her husband Gaius. Since Marcus left, he had thrown himself into his work furiously. She knew the turmoil that he was going through. As a Patrician he faced the awful prospect of not having a male child to continue the illustrious name of Metellus Cimber, descended from Scipio Africanus himself.[9] She herself was nearing the change of life; it was more and more unlikely that she would conceive another child. At the same time— which most galled her—Gaius continued to view her as he had always done: as a frivolous woman who liked parties more than him and his needs.

But she had changed. Ever since Junia's death, she had become far more reflective and serious about life: she *had* to do so. And now that Marcus had revealed that he was a Christian, and had left their home, she was on the point of despair. She realized that Gaius was all that she had left in life, and that all the new Eastern hairstylists, games, and dinner parties could not give her what she most wanted. She took a great interest in Gaius's work, and his health. She even accompanied him at times in the litter that took him to the Senate, and would afterward speak with his *clientes* (assistants) about how his economic program for the Emperor was going.

What she most feared is that he might leave her for another woman. It was so easy for a man to obtain a divorce in

[9] Famous Roman victor over Hannibal of Carthage at the battle of Zama, more than three hundred years earlier.

Rome, for the smallest reason. Though she admired Gaius's high moral principles as a Stoic, she knew that many Roman men had mistresses, or had divorced their wives for financial reasons. How much easier it would be for a younger woman to give him a child to continue his family name . . .

She had prayed for a month to Venus, the goddess of love, for fertility, and even tried a love potion that one of her friends had given her from a Persian magician. But it only made her sick, and ashamed of herself. She then began to visit Cupid's shrine every day so that her husband would find her more desirable. She stopped styling her hair with elaborate curls and folds, but wore it more simply, as she knew that he preferred.

But he continued very caught up in his own world, and practically unaware of her, except to greet her when leaving or entering their home, or answering her in very short sentences.

About two months after Marcus had left, she decided on a bold move. Just after sunset she approached his study next to the atrium. He had strewn the green marble table with several scrolls that he had received from Antoninus, and was trimming the wax lantern for more light. He had been staying up late for many evenings, and had not been coming to their bed chamber. She tapped lightly on the large oak door that had an engraving of the Roman eagle with the subscript SPQR.[10] Gaius looked up suddenly, with a look of mild irritation on his face, which she returned with the most gracious smile she could produce.

"Dear husband, I know it is late, and you have many things on your mind, but may I have a brief conversation with you?"

Her husband wanted to say no, but he compelled himself to say yes out of politeness. He invited her to sit on the chair

[10] The letters SPQR were the official insignia of the Roman government: in Latin, *Senatus Populusque Romanus*, meaning the Senate and the People of Rome.

next to the table, where he would sometimes give instructions to his *clientes*, or speak with a senator.

"I am not a Senator," Aurelia said with a soft laugh, "but I think that I have something important to say."

Gaius, who never thought that she had anything important to say, wanted to roll his eyes in disbelief, but he restrained himself. Something in his wife's bearing and tone of voice told him that now was a time to listen more carefully to her.

"I know that for years you have not had a high opinion of me, as you did for Junia," his wife began. "And I admit that for many years of our marriage I have been frivolous and thoughtless about things. Please forgive me."

Gaius smiled faintly, and only nodded his head in reply.

"Ever since Junia was killed, I've been trying to be more serious about things. Have you noticed that I hardly ever go to plays anymore, and that I am caring for things at home much more?"

Gaius had not really thought on those matters, but he had to admit that she was right. "Yes," he said hastily, while beginning to feel a little uncomfortable.

"And have you noticed over the past year that I have taken a much greater interest in your work, as Junia used to do?"

"Yes," Gaius answered, as he felt something stirring in his mind and feelings that had not stirred in a long time. It was true: Aurelia had shown a far greater interest in him, but he had been too blind to see it. Then, to his complete disconcertment, she took his right hand into both of hers and pressed it to herself. "I know, Gaius, that you desperately want a child, a male child to continue your name. It's what you're always thinking about, isn't it?"

Gaius was speechless. She had read his soul perfectly, and had articulated something that he did not want to face. She was right: what would his father Tullius have said to him if he had no son or grandson? It was a betrayal of his family heritage.

He spoke slowly, as he continued to search into her eyes. "Yes, dear wife, Junia is no more, and Marcus . . ."

"As if he were no more."

Gaius then looked away suddenly. He would have preferred to work days on the Emperor's budget than to face the question that his wife was presenting to him. But he knew that it had to be answered. For the first time in many months he actually smiled at his wife, and took her hand in his.

"I'm older now, Gaius," Aurelia said softly. "I can give you no more children, unless Venus performs a wonder. If . . ." she was beginning to sob, and took a deep breath as if she were forcing herself to say something. "If you must have a son," she continued, "I give you permission to divorce me and take another woman."

Gaius shook his head vigorously and stood up. It seemed that he was trying to clear away a thought that was greatly bothering him. He didn't answer her directly, but only groaned under his breath and said in a hoarse voice: "I loved Junia so much, and Marcus . . . Marcus has betrayed me!"

Aurelia stood up next to him, and took his hand again into hers. She couldn't agree that Marcus had betrayed him, but simply said, "Though Junia and Marcus are gone, I still love you, Gaius."

He found himself looking up into her light blue eyes, and noting her fair skin and hair in a different way. When he had first met her and fallen in love in the middle of Trajan's reign, he had often kidded her about those light features, uncommon in Rome. "Could a Goth have jumped over the fence in your family history, Aurelia?" he had once asked her teasingly, but she simply laughed and said she didn't know. He also felt a pang in his conscience as he recalled that when Marcus was only two years old, before he became a Stoic, he had had an affair with a Patrician woman, though he had never told Aurelia.

He stood up, put his arms around his wife, and kissed her twice. In his heart he felt a surge of gratitude for her honesty and fidelity to him, along with regret for not having noticed it earlier. Then taking her hand into his, they walked through the courtyard into their bed chamber. Caesar's budget could wait.

XII.

Since he had been forced to leave his home, Marcus had been praying to the Lord Christ for his parents. He knew that both of them were deeply hurt by his decision to become a Christian. He was most afraid for his father: since the days of Cato, many Stoics had chosen the path of suicide in the case of wounded honor. But Marcus was convinced that the Lord Christ, to whom he had given his entire self, would protect his father and mother. "You have to keep praying for both of them," Atticus told him, soon after he moved into the small flat near the Athenaeum. "God will bring them to himself somehow."

Marcus loved Atticus's company: he would often arrange his midday to have a meal with him and walk with him afterward. The young priest earned a living at Turibius's shop, drafting plans for the new aqueduct and bridge that Caesar planned to construct up the Tiber river—but for the rest of the day, and often during evenings, he visited Christian families, anointed the sick, and assisted Bishop Pius and his presbyters at different celebrations of the Eucharist. [11]

One Sunday, as they were leaving from the Eucharist at the Aventine house, and carrying a collection of food for the poor in their arms, Marcus asked his friend about Justus and his family, who had met Junia in the catacomb five years before.

[11] The Eucharist is from a Greek word meaning "thanksgiving," since Christians gave thanks to God at the Mass for their redemption and for the gift of his Son's body and blood.

"The last time I saw them was at Dédicus's baptism at the Easter Vigil. Do you remember?"

"Yes," said his friend. "Did you know that Constantia lost the child she was carrying at that time?"

"I had heard that. But you arrived in time to give her confirmation," Marcus added, with a little tap on his friend's shoulder.

"Thanks to Séptimus's chariot," Atticus responded laughing. And Marcus laughed to himself also at the amusing way that Atticus pronounced the word chariot, as if saying it through his nose, as the Gauls did. "But Justus and Consti now have another child."

"You mean that Consti was able to have another child?" Marcus asked with surprise.

"No, they actually went to the Via Nomentana, at the corner near the bakers' shops."

"You mean the place where people leave their unwanted children?" [12]

"Yes, Justus and Consti went there one Saturday, while you were in Egypt. They found an infant girl lying near the door of a baker's shop; it was lucky that one of the street mongrels had not gotten to her first."

"What name did they give her?"

"They named her Tertia, because they think that she was only three days old when they found her."

"They must be very happy."

"Yes they are, and they would like to invite you for dinner soon, since they heard that you were living by yourself and that you might appreciate some company."

---

[12] Though the practice diminished under the later Emperors, pagan parents would often leave deformed or unwanted children on the street corners of the city. Christian couples would regularly go and take them into their own homes.

XIII.

Within a week's time Marcus was riding on horseback to Justus's house along the Via Portuensis, with Father Atticus sitting behind him. His mother had arranged for him to use one of the horses from the family's farm, since she knew that her son loved to ride them. "Even Christians need a bit of relaxation," she had reasoned with her husband, who agreed to loan Marcus the horse. Atticus was impressed by the way his friend handled the animal; it was a smooth and pleasant ride from the city to Justus's house.

The country villa had changed a little since Marcus had seen it at Dedicus's baptism a few years before, when he had met Bishop Telesphorus for the first time, who later died so gloriously for Christ. There was a large bright mosaic on the atrium's left wall, with the image of a red-gold sun rising over the blue sea, and a small white sailing ship in the distance. It reminded Marcus of the sailing ships on Marcia's and Junia's tombs, and on other Christian graves that he had seen in Alexandria.

"Justus," Marcus said as he greeted the big man with a Roman armshake, "you've collected a few denarii since I saw you last. What a beautiful mosaic . . ."

"That was really Carmina's idea," Justus answered, shrugging his broad shoulders. "She's the artist of the house."

"And where is the newest arrival to the family?" the son of Gaius asked.

Justus led them to the room closest to the atrium, near a little stone fountain. Consti was bouncing the little girl on her lap, and teasing her with a small colored rattle.

She recognized Marcus immediately as he entered.

"Marcus," she said with a smile. "You're always welcome in this house, at any time. We know about the trouble you've had with your father and mother."

"I appreciate the offer, Constantia, but actually my lectures at the Athenaeum keep me pretty busy—and I always get great support from the fellows at the house on the Aventine."

"I bet you miss Numer and Dédicus."

Marcus bowed his head, and shuffled his feet self-consciously. Yes, he really did miss them. *How do women read minds so easily?*

At that moment Carmina entered the room, with a small container of milk for Tertia. Marcus was amazed at the change in her. At only fifteen she had become a lovely young woman, with light brown hair like her mother, but a darker color of skin like her father. There was a true gracefulness in the way she walked, and she greeted Marcus with a bashful smile. He had remembered her as the little girl with the flute at the reception after Dédicus's and Cynthia's baptism.

"Carmina," Marcus asked her with an inquisitive grin, "do you still play the flute and the lyre?"

"Oh, yes," she answered, lowering her eyes a bit as she handed the container of milk to Constantia, "but I like to sing, more."

"She has a beautiful voice," her mother said, "she teaches hymns to the children before the Eucharist here every week. And she often leads the singing of one of the Psalms before the bishop proclaims the Gospel."

Carmina blushed a little as everyone looked at her. She didn't know what to say, and was relieved when her brother Timotheus entered the room. He still had a slight stoop, and could not walk very steadily, because of the knife wounds that Odius and his gang gave him at school four years before. He was in obvious pain as he walked in, but managed to give Marcus a broad smile and shook his hand.

"What happened on your trip to Alexandria, Marcus? Did you meet any pirates on the way?"

"No," Marcus joked, "Pompey [13] did a pretty a good job on

[13] The Roman General Pompey defeated the pirates who had infested the Mediterranean around the year 60 B.C.; since then, the Romans termed this body of water *Mare Nostrum*, "our sea."

them a few years back, but there were a lot of seagulls that squealed at me, and one left a dropping on my red cape."

They all laughed at that one, after which Justus invited them to the triclinium,[14] where supper was prepared. Since Marcus was at his house last, Justus had had some success in his business, and had hired a cook for the family named Tullianus, who originally came from Spain. He, too, was a Christian, a young man with a dark complexion and a serious look on his face. He didn't live with the family, but walked from the city each day, then returned home after supper to take care of his mother, who lived in one of the flats near the old forum. Once a week Consti invited both of them to supper; Justus or Carmina would drive them from the city, and they themselves would serve Tullianus and his mother a special meal.

At the end of *cena*, Marcus asked if they could say a prayer for his father and mother, so that they would find the Lord Christ someday. They all walked into the atrium and knelt toward the East, toward Jerusalem, making the sign of the cross on their foreheads, lips, and chests. It was around the eleventh hour of the day. After Atticus led them in prayer, Carmina brought her lyre and sang a little hymn for everyone:

> *O Lord Jesus Christ,*
> *Our treasure is in You;*
> *No matter what the pain or cost*
> *We shall be your witness true.*
> *One heart, one mind, one soul*
> *We are all one Body in You;*
> *No matter what the pain or cost*
> *We shall be your witness true.*

---

[14] The Roman dining room, where people reclined to eat on couches, usually three persons per couch.

"That's a beautiful hymn, Carmina," Atticus said. "Did you compose it?"

"I composed the music, but Timo gave me the words."

Going back to Rome, Marcus rode the horse at a slower pace, so that he could speak better with Atticus, sitting behind him. "That was a brave smile that Timo gave me; I could see that he was in pain."

"He has his ups and downs," the young priest answered. "At times he gets depressed, but he always manages to look his best when guests come."

"Is he able to work?"

"He helps his father repairing the fish carts—Justus recently bought two more, with two more horses, since his business is expanding. Timo also takes care of the horses; he's quite good with them. In his free time he reads, especially Cicero."

"Do you think he will ever become an attorney?"

"He has two strikes against him for that," Atticus answered. "He's a Christian, and he really can't study for any length of time, because he gets tired."

Marcus spurred the young mare a bit harder as he passed a carriage on the side of the road. "The Lord gave him a cross at a very young age," he said. "I suppose that he is unable to marry."

"I doubt that he would be able to marry. But despite his ailment, he seems happy enough just being with his family, and trying to help them in little ways. He's very good at whittling, and gives small wooden figures and other gifts to people from his art."

"What about Carmina? Does she have any plans?"

"Carmina is thinking to marry fairly soon."

"Yes, she's about the right age. She'll be a melodious prize for some lucky fellow," Marcus observed. "Is she thinking of someone?"

"Oh, yes," Atticus answered, "and you've met him. He's

Gaius, son of Discalus the fish merchant. They've known each other since they were children; Gaius is Timo's best friend. He and Carmina have often been seen walking in the park near the baths of Neptune, and they seem to care for each other very much."

XIV.

Marcus and Atticus arrived to the city shortly after sunset, when the streets became a moving mass of carts, horses, and curses. Atticus walked to his small tenement apartment near Trajan's forum, where Father Eusebius was waiting up for him.

"How was your day, Eusebius?" Atticus asked.

"Bishop Pius moved around quite a bit today, from one end of the city to the other. There was a Eucharist at a house near the Temple of Isis, instructions for a large group of catechumens meeting in Dorca's atrium, then anointings of the sick in the Subura district. I also heard several confessions."

"You must be tired," Atticus rejoined with a bit of envy in his voice. Eusebius, who was originally from Antioch, and whose father had known Paul himself, was Pius's main assistant, and accompanied him on most of his sacramental journeys.

"I'm a little tired, yes . . ." the older man said, but his words were cut short by a cart screeching outside of their window, mixed with the sound of curses.

It was getting colder, so Atticus put a log in the iron stove in the corner, being careful to close the grate so the sparks wouldn't fly. Tenement houses were real fire traps, and many Christians had lost friends and relatives to fires in the poorer neighborhoods. Atticus went to a narrow couch at one side of the room, and prepared to go to sleep.

He had composed a prayer in Gallic to the Mother of the Lord Christ, which he often said at night after praying the

Nunc Dimittis.[15] The brief prayer asked the Virgin Mary for purity in thought and body, and also for a sound sleep at night.

But the carts and noises were particularly loud that night, and he couldn't get to sleep right away. For some reason he could not stop thinking of Carmina, whom he had just seen at Justus's house. What a beautiful hymn she had sung! What an attractive young woman she had become, with those clear signs of womanhood showing beneath her light blue tunic. Without wanting it, he felt something impure stirring in him, and shook his head vigorously, trying to drive it away. Then he laughed a little at himself and whispered, *Oh, Atticus, there you go again. Poor vessel of clay that you are, don't forget that you're carrying a treasure.* But since he continued to be tempted in his thoughts, he got up briefly and walked quietly around the room. *"Ave Maria Puríssima,"* he repeated slowly, and then, kneeling down he silently prayed, "O Lord Christ, I give myself to you once more for the hundredfold, the pearl of great price."[16] After a few minutes he went back to his couch, but still could not sleep.

He began to reflect on his younger years growing up in Gaul, just north of Lyons.

He had been born of a Christian family; his father owned a small farm with some sheep and horses. He had loved the quiet country life, but when he was eighteen he felt drawn to go to Rome to study architecture. His father encouraged him to go, and gave him a small amount of money to get started at Turibius's school. It was while at school that he met Numer, who had also begun his study of philosophy at the Athenaeum, though he was a bit older than Atticus. He was immediately impressed by Numer, not

---

[15] The prayer of Simeon at the presentation of Christ in the Temple of Jerusalem (see Lk 2: 29–32).

[16] The Gospel passage on the pearl of great price (Mt 13: 46) primarily refers to making a full commitment to God's Kingdom, and can therefore apply to all dedicated Christian men and women—but in a special way it has been applied in Church history to those who have received the gift of celibacy.

only for his intelligence and sense of humor, but for the depth of his faith. He dreamed of converting the whole city of Rome to Christ, and from there the whole world. If he faced some obstacle or misunderstanding, he would invariably quote the Master's sayings about the leaven in the mass and the mustard seed. "We can't give up, Atticus, we can't give up. It's going to work, you'll see, just like the mustard seed and the leaven."

Little by little he and Atticus met other students, most of them non-Christians . . . but through friendship and God's grace they had been able to win over many of them to Christ. Pooling their resources, they were able to purchase the house on the Aventine Hill, where he and Numer lived with Titus and five other Christian students. The atrium was quite large and served not only for the Sunday Eucharist, when different families came from nearby for the Lord's sacrifice, but also for classes that Numer and Titus gave; at other times it served simply for gatherings where they and their friends would talk about things, or sing and play music on important days. Atticus particularly remembered Numer's flute and Titus' poem in his honor on the day he graduated from Turibius's school. That was the day that Dédicus had first brought Marcus to meet them all.

Somehow, through those friendships and conversations, God had given him the grace to think of the priesthood. He began to meet with some of the presbyters in Rome, especially Nicanor from Crete, who had introduced him to Bishop Telesphorus. While studying architecture, he also received personal training from Nicanor on preaching the Lord's Gospel, understanding the writings of Paul and others, and administering of the sacraments. Shortly after Junia was killed, he had been ordained by Telesphorus at the young age of twenty-three. It was the most wonderful day in his life, and his parents had come from Gaul for the ceremony.

"You must now pray especially for your son, that he be

holy and faithful to the Lord Christ," the Pope had told his parents, who were both weeping.

Atticus rose from the couch, and walked softly again around the narrow room. He admired Eusebius's ability to sleep so soundly, despite the noise from the street. Then again, he was from Antioch, which also had very loud noises at night, like Rome. The older priest was a married man, but upon being ordained in Antioch, he had left his home with the consent of his wife, a Christian from Laodicea. She had then joined a group of Christian women in Antioch, as the wives of so many presbyters had done since the time of the Apostles. His children were all grown by then, and had been raised in the faith of Christ. Eusebius told Atticus that one of his daughters had just married a Christian from Ephesus.

Suddenly there was the sound of a brawl outside; it was a couple of drunken men fighting in front of their door. He could hear them cursing at each other about a bet they had made. He felt like going out and trying to stop it, but then considered that the best thing he could do was to kneel down and pray for them.

Yes, he thought, and *I need prayers, too.* So young and a priest. He recalled that day when he had gone to the Bishop of Rome and told him directly that he wanted to be a priest. Telesphorus had smiled.

"So young, and wanting to be a presbyter?"

"But John the apostle of Christ was also a presbyter, Holy Father, and he was even younger than I," Atticus had answered Peter's successor in a respectful, but sincere voice.

Telesphorus had nodded his head gravely at that point, then put his hands on both of his shoulders. Within three months he ordained him at the Aventine house.

XV.

The next day, returning from his lectures at the Athenaeum, Marcus found a scroll with a brown wax seal in front of his door. Some messenger had left it, perhaps one of the fellows from the Aventine. It had a few tears and scratches on it, but from the quality of the papyrus he could tell it was from one of the Eastern provinces. Marcus's heart skipped a beat when he saw that it was from Dédicus.

Vale, Marcus, what a joy to be able to write you at last. For the last few months I have been working with Justin in Ephesus. We share the same tongue and mentality, being from Samaria, as you know. I've been helping him promote his dialogue with Trypho among Christians and Jews here, which answers so many of the Jews' objections to our faith. So far it's been a success, though he has also made quite a few enemies. So it has to be, as the Lord Christ himself predicted.

But here is the good news, which I'm sure you will find exciting. Justin has decided to go to Rome. Numer and I have been speaking about it with him for over a year. He already has many disciples here in the East, including Antioch and Alexandria, and now he feels that God is calling him to the capital of the Empire. He knows that our people are being persecuted there, as everywhere, and wants to write an Apology to the Emperor on their behalf. He would particularly like to open some kind of school or academy to teach the coherence between Greek philosophy and Christian teachings. He has also heard that the Gnostics are setting up schools there. . . .

Numer and I are hoping that you will welcome him. Perhaps he could stay for a time at the Aventine House, or at some other house near those of the Way.

We expect to reach Puteoli some time in the middle of August. I'll be traveling with him, and will introduce him to you. It will be wonderful to see you again.

Are your ribs still aching from that tackle that I gave you?

Your friend in Christ, Dédicus

Marcus's heart was pounding as he read the letter. He had been waiting for this day. Apart from Servianus, who was not yet a Christian, he was the only philosopher in Rome who believed in Christ. He had to be very cautious in expounding his ideas in class, sticking literally to Plato's written text, without pointing to any deeper truth that it might be implying, almost like a man who was reading a poem but could not say the last verse. But now he would have an intellectual support in his effort, and what a support! Justin himself . . .

Marcus remembered his first encounter with him almost seven years earlier at Strabo's Institute. He had been a great lecturer, and had tantalized himself and others with his survey of philosophy that led to a Logos that was the cause of the entire universe, and a redeemer as well. Junia had warned him against Justin at first, since the approach was so Christian! But his own skepticism had gotten the better of him, especially when Justin began speaking of Jesus as the Christ, the man of miracles who rose from the dead. He was still amazed at how God had changed his mind so completely after he met Dédicus and his friends.

He made immediate plans to meet Justin and Dédicus around the ides of August, and told Titus and the fellows at the Aventine House, who were delighted at the news. He also told Servianus, who managed to get a *raeda* and two horses for the journey to Puteoli, with enough room for Justin and Dédicus to return with them to Rome. The plan was for Justin to stay for a while with Numer's friends at the Aventine, but then to find another place in Rome where he could teach and meet with students.

XVI.

The port at Puteoli was busy during the entire month of August. There were grain and passenger ships coming from different parts of the Empire, especially from North Africa,

Spain, and the Eastern Provinces. A few of the ships had up to two hundred passengers, and in one of these Justin and Dédicus arrived on the ides of August. As they walked down the broad wooden plank to the dock, Marcus of course recognized Dédicus at once. Tall, with dark straight hair and an intense look on his face, his friend walked slightly in front of his older companion. Marcus had met Justin some years earlier in Rome; he was of medium height with a round face and very observant eyes, looking keenly around him as he walked down to the dock. He had a few gray hairs now, and was wearing a pallium.[17] In Athens and Alexandria he had seen a few men wearing that same garment, but here—Marcus thought excitedly—here was the philosopher who had written so many famous papers and had defended Christianity throughout Asia.

After giving Marcus and Servianus big embraces, Dédicus introduced Justin to them.

"Dédicus has told me all about you," Justin said to Marcus as soon as he saw him.

"I hope that you remember me," Marcus replied, "I was one among twenty students who heard you at the Strabo Institute, near the Athenaeum, on your first visit here."

"Yes, I do remember you," Justin smiled ironically. "You asked the most difficult questions."

"I'm happy to report that over the last five years the Lord's Spirit has answered them for me, or at least most of them."

"I may have a few for you though," Servianus interjected with a short laugh. "I am not yet a Christian."

"The more the better," Justin answered, as if Servianus had challenged him to a boxing match. Marcus noted that the philosopher spoke excellent Latin, almost without an accent.

When they reached Rome, all the fellows at the Aventine House were waiting for them: three had actually run to meet

[17] A garment of fleece worn around the neck and on the chest, signifying a philosopher.

them just outside of the city. It was later in the day, toward the fifteenth hour, and there were oil lanterns set in front of the door, along with three large torches in the atrium. Nobody seemed to want to go to the bed, and Justin, even after his long trip from Puteoli, was delighted to meet his Christian brethren and speak with them. None of them were training to be philosophers, except Marcus and Servianus. They had all kinds of questions about how Justin had discovered Christ; though the main parts of his conversion were widely known, they delighted in hearing it again. Servianus asked him more directly about his latest writing, the *Dialogue with Trypho* the Jew.

"Why is it," he asked, "that Christians are persecuted because of their belief in the one God, but the Jews and Samaritans are not?"

"I'm afraid that we are viewed as more of a threat; even though both Jews and Christians believe there is one God, we actually believe that this one God became a man. That is perceived to be a scandal, and a danger to the Emperors. Also, we are new on the scene, and don't have the history or influence of the Jews, whose religion has long been tolerated by the Romans."

They asked Justin quite a few other questions, including how best to defend themselves against popular ideas that Christians were superstitious, or immoral, or enemies of Rome.

"It is the non-Christians who are immoral; many of them worship demons. When I can get established here a little, I will try to write an Apologeticum, a defense of our beliefs. I hope that many of you can give me ideas."

Marcus had some deeper questions involving the Logos in Greek philosophy, and its relationship to the Logos Son of God, but he thought that it was better to discuss these later with Justin. The night was progressing and people needed to rest. Before leaving though he asked Justin briefly how Numer was doing.

"While I've been in Ephesus, Numer has been working with students at the Platonic Academy in Alexandria. Besides his classes and explanations, he continues to make friends very quickly. He has brought many of them to Christ already."

"We've missed him dearly here," Philius answered. "Tell us, Dédicus, does he still joke around a lot?"

"Though I've been in Ephesus with Justin, I've heard that he continues to joke around as he teaches, with his word and with his flute . . ."

They all laughed at that, and so ended the conversation for the evening. Some of them went back to their rooms at the Aventine; others like Marcus and Servianus went back to their houses. Titus took Justin to his quarters, a fairly spacious chamber to the right of the courtyard with a large writing table. As he left, Marcus said a prayer of thanksgiving to the angels who had brought Justin and Dédicus safely to them all, but he was concerned about Titus, who still seemed distant from the others and self-absorbed.

XVII.

The day after Justin arrived, Titus went to see Fabulanus, who lived near the Subura district and was a good friend of one of the Consuls. He was a short pudgy man with a habitually soiled toga, but one of the most powerful men in Rome politically. The popular saying went, "if you know Fabulanus, you will do fabulously." As Titus entered the small house, a slave met him with a platter of figs and a goblet of cheap wine. Fabulanus came in shortly afterward. He did not waste any time.

"Titus Valerius, from the noble line of Pulcher, greetings," he said, as he bowed his head somewhat mockingly. Titus liked the salutation however. It was true that he was a Patrician, descended from noble lineage like Marcus, though as a Christian he had tried not to distinguish himself, nor give it much importance. Still, it was pleasing to hear his family title spoken.

"I heard that you might be interested in a quaestorship, Titus. Are you twenty-five yet?"[18]

"Yes," the young man answered, "I am twenty-seven."

"Do you have any experience in finance or the law?"

"I studied law under Pontianus, and worked at the bank of Diodorus for three years."

"Diodorus?" Fabulanus looked at him suspiciously. "Wasn't he killed in the amphitheater with his daughter a few years ago, for the crime of being a Christian?"

Titus turned his glance from him for a moment, and fidgeted a bit with the edge of his carefully folded and clean toga. "Yes, he was a Christian, but his banking service was considered to be the best in Rome, and he always conducted himself with scrupulous honesty."

"I know that," Fabulanus answered hastily, as if it really didn't matter how honest he was. "But tell me, Master Titus, are you also a Christian?"

"Working for a Christian does not make you one."

"Answer my question. Are you a member of the Christian cult or not?"

Titus bit the bottom of his lip. He had been afraid of that question, but had not wanted to face it.

"Absolutely not," Titus said loudly, but he couldn't look Fabianus in the eye as he said it, and he felt blood rushing to his head.

"Good," Fabulanus answered. "Now let's get on to other matters. You are a fairly good speaker; did you study Rhetoric?"

"Yes, for two years at the Athenaeum," Titus answered in a low voice, still trembling on the inside for the false answer he had just given.

"You have a good appearance. Perhaps something can be done for you, for a good enough fee. The Emperor wants

[18] Caesar Augustus lowered the minimum age for the office of quaestor from thirty to twenty-five.

competent financial assistants, who can argue their case well before the Senators and the Tribunes. Do you have any money?"

"Not much. As you may have heard, my father had to sell our estate near Capua to pay off some debts."

Fabulanus narrowed his eyes a bit and grinned. "That's all right," he said. "Let's see how you handle yourself in the weeks ahead. You must do exactly what I tell you. If you're appointed quaestor, you can take care of my fee, and then some."

As Titus left the small house, he was shaking his head sadly. Why did he have to lie? What would his grandparents have said, who were one of the first Patrician couples converted by Kephas eighty years earlier? Yet the quaestorship would be a key position, he thought, from which he could spread the message of Christ. It would be a unique opportunity for the whole Christian community, which was so despised and misunderstood by everyone. He would have power and influence, since everyone knew that the quaestorship was the first qualifying step toward becoming a Senator . . . yes, power and influence to do good, he kept telling himself, though he was doubtful of his real motivation.

His conscience bothered him as he returned to the Domus Aventina. He tried to smile as he entered the atrium, where he saw Pellus and Sextus speaking energetically with Justin. He went quickly to his room to the left of the courtyard, and lay down on his couch. He was very sorry for his momentary weakness, and he determined to go to one of the presbyters as soon as possible, and confess his sin. He prayed that he would not be given a severe public penance, or expelled from the Eucharist, since he had not publicly denied the Lord Christ.[19]

[19] In the early Church the sin of apostasy (denying belief in Christ, and offering sacrifice to the pagan gods) was considered to be the gravest of sins. Expulsion from the Eucharist and severe penance lasting for years were often given by bishops to those who had publicly denied their faith in Christ. They were called the *lapsi*, or "fallen ones."

XVIII.

Months passed, and Titus was gaining support among both Patricians and Plebeians. He and another Christian named Philius had joined an advocacy group that protected the rights of some poorer families in Rome. Though Titus had done this to follow the Master's way of charity, it also had the effect of enhancing his reputation for a larger part of the population. He was a good speaker, and carefully promoted the Emperor's fiscal reforms. He even spoke with Gaius, Marcus's father, for ways that he could present the Emperor's program more effectively to the groups he was addressing. Gaius suspected that he was a Christian, but said nothing.

By September he was almost assured of the Consul's support for nomination as a quaestor, which always took place on the fifth of December. Marcus was delighted at the prospect, as were the other fellows at the Domus Aventina. He had written to Dédicus, who had returned to Ephesus by then, and to Numer in Alexandria, asking for their prayers. But at the same time he was concerned for Titus's safety. If he rose to such a high office, he would become an obvious target for political enemies because of his religion.

On a fine sunny day just after the calends[20] of September, Marcus walked up the familiar hill to join his friends for the afternoon meal, after he had finished lecturing at the Athenaeum. To his surprise he saw Philius nervously pacing up and down the courtyard in front of the house. It reminded him of the day he that saw Numer doing the same, just after Bishop Telesphorus had been arrested.

"What's wrong, Philius?" the young philosopher asked his friend.

"The worst has come to pass, Marcus—what we all feared."

"Is it about Titus?"

[20] The calends are the first day of the month.

"Yes, one of his rivals for the office of quaestor, Antigonus of Capua, has accused him of being a Christian."

At that point Marcus said a word under his breath that his father would not have liked.

Philius heard it, gave him a sympathetic smile, then continued: "There will surely be a trial, and all of Titus's rights will be protected—this Emperor has been good about that with us, you know—but the evidence is pretty clear against him. There are two or three eyewitnesses, all Roman citizens, who saw him going to a Eucharist in the catacomb along the Via Appia. What's more, all of us living here have come under suspicion because of it. It's pretty well known that groups of Christians come to this house regularly, especially on Sundays."

"The Master predicted that this would happen, didn't he?" Marcus said softly.

"Yes," replied Philius, "and we're prepared to suffer with him if God wants it so, but we're praying that he'll be able to escape the charge in some way. As you recall, it was he, Numer, and Atticus that actually began this house."

Marcus said nothing; he too was prepared to suffer for the Lord Christ at any time, though he realized that he was not in as much danger as Titus's friends at the house. He and Philius knelt down facing the East, toward Jerusalem, and prayed for Titus together. They might have to find a place quickly for Justin to move, and Marcus already had an idea of where it could be.

Marcus and Philius went to Titus's trial, which took place in an ancient courtroom near the Temple of Jupiter, on the Capitoline Hill. The judge was a well-known Stoic named Lucullus. When Marcus heard it was he, he was not sure what to think, since Lucullus was known throughout the city for his rigorous fairness, which could work either for or against Titus. In the previous year Lucullus had denounced two men who had tried to bribe him; that had created a great sensation in Rome, since judges rarely refused bribes.

The two witnesses against Titus gave their testimonies first. One claimed to have seen him coming from a Christian catacomb along the Via Appia early in the morning, on the second day before the ides of July, accompanied by two men he didn't know. He also had overheard them speaking of the Christian superstition called the Eucharist, though he didn't hear the exact words. The other claimed that he had seen Titus frequently coming from a certain house on the Aventine Hill, which was highly suspected of being a gathering place for Christian families. On the next day the prosecution actually produced a third witness who had worked at Diodorus's bank as a clerk for many years; he claimed that on several occasions he had overheard Titus and Diodorus—a Christian from Corinth who had been condemned to death with his daughter Marcia several years earlier—speaking about Jesus Christ.

Though Marcus was not trained in Law, he was greatly troubled by the evidence against Titus. The witnesses were calm and very articulate, though he later learned that two of them were actually hired spies. He could only listen and pray, as did Philius next to him. As the trial progressed, it seemed more and more likely that Titus would be convicted.

But then a most astonishing thing occurred which Marcus would remember for the rest of his life. Titus's attorney, who had been strangely silent during the first part of the trial and had made no objections, suddenly began questioning the witnesses in a way that completely reversed the direction of the proceeding. A small man with a round face and shining dark eyes (Marcus never learned his name), he began to undermine the case of the prosecution against Titus. To the witness who claimed that he saw Titus coming from the catacomb he asked if the mere fact of seeing a man coming from a catacomb makes him a Christian, or even the fact of speaking about the Christian practice of the Eucharist. "Many in Rome have heard and speak of the Christian practice called the Eucharist," he stated, "but that does not make them Christians: and remember, sir, that you can't even reproduce his words, or their context," he added for emphasis. To the witness who saw Titus going and coming from the house on the Aventine, he asked if frequent visits could really prove anything about Titus's religion; perhaps he had some regular business there, or even had a friend there, whom he was trying to dissuade from being a Christian. To the one who overheard Titus and Diodorus speaking about Christ he used the same line of questioning: the mere fact of hearing a conversation about Jesus Christ does not make either of them a Christian. Diodorus had been condemned as a Christian because he and his daughter had refused to offer wine and incense to the Emperor's statue, not because he had spoken about Christ to a friend. "Besides," he added, "it's a fact that many Romans talk about Christians and Christ all the time. Why should Titus's words about Christ be held against him, especially since he is on trial for his life?"

The prosecutor objected and appealed to Lucullus the judge. He presented arguments and counter-arguments for two days, but he was unable to re-establish the credibility of his witnesses or his case against Titus. Given the fact that the Emperor had set clear standards of proof for all trials against Christians, and Lucullus's reputation for absolute fairness, Titus was acquitted. Marcus and Philius ran up to him and embraced him, and the word quickly spread among the entire Christian community in Rome. *Gratias tibi agimus, Domine* (we give you thanks, O Lord) was the prayer of many of them, as they kissed one another for joy, recalling the joy of those earlier followers of the Way who rejoiced when Peter and John were released from prison.[21]

Titus trembled when his acquittal was pronounced, and he began to weep in his chair. During the entire ordeal he feared that he would not have the courage to admit that he

[21] See Acts 4: 23–25.

was a Christian, if he were forced to answer that question in public. Now he was to be spared that agonizing choice which so many hundreds of Christians before him had been forced to face: *renounce your belief in Christ, offer wine and incense to the Roman gods—or die.*

As he walked back to his home with his two friends, he was strangely silent. He was deeply sorry for the lie he told to Fabulanus; he had had good intentions, and had received absolution for his sin of weakness, but he never realized that the matter would reach this point of crisis. He saw very clearly that the house on the Aventine would have to be closed. It had served its purpose, but it was now under a heavy cloud of suspicion. Any person living there would be immediately suspected as a Christian, and more spies could be hired. There would be more accusations, and more trials. They had opened it seven years earlier with such enthusiasm, but now he felt that he had to make a decision for the good of everyone.

He knew that his political career was ruined, because Rome was a city of constant gossip and innuendo: people's reputation could be destroyed in a day. He would have to talk with Marcus, and find a place for Justin to live. His important work had to continue, especially since a couple of dangerous intellectuals had just appeared on the scene in Rome: Marcion of Sinope, and Valentinus, a Gnostic disciple of Basilides. Numer had written to them about these men, warning that they could deceive many of the faithful with their ideas.

As he and his friends passed by Discalus's old fish stand on the Via Biberatica, Titus stopped suddenly.

"Wait," he said, as if waking from a troubled dream, "I never did find out the name of that attorney who defended me so brilliantly. I barely had a chance to speak with him before the trial, and he left the courtroom as soon as it was ended. I was never able to thank him. I don't even know where he was from . . ."

"I've been thinking about that," Philius said, "and I believe that I have the answer."

"What do you mean?" both Titus and Marcus asked him with one voice.

"Isn't that the sort of thing that angels do?"

XIX.

Like Titus, Cynthia had joined a philanthropic group that took care of orphaned children.[22] Every Saturday she volunteered at a large house at the foot of the Janiculum, which was used to house street children . . . boys and girls of all ages, who had nowhere to go. Cynthia helped to prepare their meals, played games with them, and took care of them if they were sick. She also gave lessons in grammar and pronunciation, since many of them could not even speak their native Latin well.

Almost every day now Cynthia visited Scintilla in her small apartment at the edge of the Subura district, as she continued to decline in health. Statira fixed her meals, and Frieda stayed overnight with her, sleeping on the couch at the other side of the room. On Friday evenings several of them would gather at her place to sing and tell her amusing stories, or ask her to pray for their friends whom they were trying to bring to the Lord Christ. They also loved to ask her questions about her early days in Rome, since she had known people converted by Peter and Paul themselves.

"Last time you talked about Eunice and Mary Magdalene, but tell us how you found the Lord Christ and joined the Church."

"Oh, but I've told you those things already, many times," Scintilla answered.

"Tell us again," they insisted, "or about your days in Gallia."

[22] Under the Emperor Antoninus Pius (A.D. 138–161), many of these foundations for the poor were begun in Rome.

She said she was from a little village in central Gaul that had a camp of Roman soldiers nearby. Her father was a merchant, and would be gone for many days at a time. Her mother died when she was young; she was an only child. Her father's new wife was rather cruel to her, and often ignored her. As a young woman of seventeen, she was tall with attractive dark hair; she used to hide in a neighbor's barn when the soldiers came to the village so that they wouldn't molest her, or take her as a slave to Rome. But one day a soldier saw her running away and followed her into the barn. Scintilla said this only once, with tears in her eyes. Everyone knew what happened; she didn't have to say any more. A few years afterward she was taken to Rome and sold on the market as a kitchen slave.

Her first mistress was the wife of a quaestor at the beginning of Trajan's reign. She was very demanding, and often beat her with a stick.

"But that house was really lucky for me," Scintilla continued, "because there I met Chloë, the little girl from Syria. She first started telling me, as we worked in the kitchen, about the Master and his teachings, and the fact that he had risen from the dead, and would raise up all who believed in him."

"Did you believe her?" Portia asked, who had come with Cynthia that day; she was not yet baptized.

"Not at first, little one," the old woman answered, looking away and coughing a bit. "I had never heard of such a thing, though there were many superstitions in Gallia about spirits of the dead coming back to haunt people. But she seemed so enthusiastic and sincere about Christ that I had to listen to her, since she would always talk about him. She also told me that Christ was coming soon in something called the *parousia*, so that I had better hurry up and believe."

Some of them laughed at that, while others, including Scintilla, were more serious.

"But she was so kind to me," Scintilla continued, "and

with such good humor that I couldn't turn her down. So I went to some meetings with her and other Christians at the house of Tullus, who was an importer of olives and had a large house near the fountain of Mercury. That's where I was baptized."

"That's pretty close to Marcia's house," Cynthia interjected.

Scintilla coughed again, and asked for a bit of water.

"Yes, it was as God wanted. One day, about fifteen years after I was baptized, I saw Marcia's father Diodorus, who was a widower then, at one of the meetings. He had moved from Corinth to Rome two years earlier, and had established his bank with a partner from Thessalonica. He was a short, stocky man, I remember, always smiling and bowing to everyone."

"That's how I'll always remember him, but his mannerisms annoyed Junia a little," Cynthia said.

"Yes, but that's getting ahead of the story. In Corinth Diodorus and Helena had a hard time conceiving a child, though they wanted one with all of their heart. They prayed and prayed, and finally the Lord gave them a daughter, a cute little thing with freckles and red hair. But Helena died of an illness when Marcia was only three, and Diodorus took her to Rome to begin a new life here. After meeting me at Tullus's house and knowing that I was a Christian, he purchased me from the quaestor—I was so happy to get away from that woman!—and placed me with the kitchen servants. Almost all of them were Christians, too."

Scintilla asked at that point if someone could put a little more wood in the iron stove near her chair. It seemed that she was always cold. She coughed a bit, got up and walked a few steps, then sat down again.

After a little while, when Scintilla was more rested, Cynthia asked her about Marcia.

"She was so much fun to be with, always singing and playing tricks on people, like a little red fox. But she would become very serious at times, especially when she said her prayers to the Lord Christ and his mother."

"We all know that Junia was her best friend."

"Yes, it was wonderful to see them together. They were so different really: Junia, tall, beautiful, dignified . . . and Marcia short, with a plain freckled face, and full of pranks."

"They're both with God now," Portia said solemnly.

"You're right, little one, and I think I'll be joining them soon."

"Oh, no, Scintilla, don't say that," Portia answered as she rose from the floor, bent over her and gave her a little kiss on the cheek. "We need you here."

"Tell us about how you and Marcia decided to give yourself completely to the Savior," Frieda asked her, hoping to continue the conversation a while longer, since they were all enjoying it so much.

"Oh, you all want to know too much," Scintilla said.

"Nooooo . . ." they all shouted together. "Tell us . . . ," they pleaded with her.

"Well it was right after I moved to the house of Diodorus. I had been thinking about the hundredfold and the pearl of great price for some time; I had met many women in the city who had chosen that path, like Eunice and the first holy women who followed Christ. But the enthusiastic little kitchen slave from Syria helped me the most, the one who introduced me to Christ, and took me to see Ignatius's great sacrifice in the Colosseum many years before."

"What ever happened to her?" Cynthia asked.

"She was thrown to the beasts at the beginning of Hadrian's reign, about the time that Marcia and Junia were born. She was completely calm about the whole terrible thing; when she walked into the arena, she was even singing a hymn from her village that she had learned as a child. Everyone in the stadium was cursing her and Christ. That helped me to decide that the only thing worth living for, and dying for, was the love of Christ. A few freed men later wanted to have me in marriage. I guess I was attractive then," she added with a little grimace, "but I turned them down. I knew that Jesus and his Way were the love of my life, and no man could ever fill that, whether freed or slave."

"And what about Marcia? When did she decide?" Sabina asked.

"One of Marcia's earliest memories of her mother was to hear her singing, then praying with her; Helena at that time would tell her, in very simple terms, about the pearl of great price, and the joy of giving up everything for Christ. It made a huge impression on Marcia, and when her mother died shortly afterward, that impression became confirmed even more in her soul. When the little girl saw that I was giving up marriage for Christ, she wanted it for herself. Marcia and I were very close, despite the difference in our ages." As she said this, Scintilla's voice cracked a bit, and she began to sob. It was obvious to them all how much she had loved that little girl from Corinth, whom Junia had also loved.

Everyone was silent for a moment, and prayed with her. It was at that moment that they all heard a sound of rushing wind in the room, though the windows and doors were closed. One of them began speaking for several moments in tongues,[23] and they could feel a divine Presence in the room: it was the Holy Spirit. Nobody could understand the girl who was speaking, though Cynthia recognized a few words in Greek. It didn't matter . . . they could all feel her joy. Many of them knelt down and made the sign of the cross on their forehead, lips, and breast.

It was hard for anyone to speak for a while after that. But finally Statira summoned up the courage to ask Scintilla the next question.

---

[23] This charism is called *glossolaly*, a grace given to many of the faithful in the early Church, and in subsequent centuries. The first instance of this grace—also called gift of tongues—is recorded with the coming of the Holy Spirit upon the Apostles in Acts 2: 1–13. In that case, the meaning was intelligible to all.

"And what about Bishop Telesphorus? When did you meet him?"

"That was one of my happiest moments," Scintilla answered. "The Lord's spirit moved me to volunteer with a group of women who were serving Bishop Telesphorus and some of his presbyters. They took care of their meals and cleaned the house where they were staying, not far from the Vatican Hill, where Peter lies. As I told you before, I felt part of that great tradition which began with Mary the Mother of Jesus, Mary Magdalene, and Salomé. They gave up everything to serve Jesus and his apostles. I wish I could continue to serve the Holy Father Pius, but I'm too old now."

"No, Scintilla, you're the youngest among us," Cynthia countered, with the sharp wit that came from her Greek background.

"Now you're teasing me," Scintilla answered, then continued speaking. "It was an extra burden for me and the others when the Bishop asked if we could help the group of young men living at the house on the Aventine, but it was not far from the house of Diodorus, and we could do it by organizing ourselves a little more. We knew that they too had given up everything for the Lord Christ, and were trying to be his apostles in Rome."

XX.

A week later Scintilla died peacefully, in her sleep. Bishop Pius with all the presbyters in the city celebrated the Eucharist for her in the atrium of Marius's house; it was overflowing with many kinds of people, both slaves and free, whom Scintilla had touched with her prayer and example. She was laid to rest for the Lord's coming in the same catacomb in which Marcia and Junia were buried, in a *loculus* [24] only a few feet away from them. Painted on her tombstone was the

[24] *Loculus* is a niche in the walls of the catacombs where the bodies of the deceased were placed, then sealed up.

image of a golden field of wheat, and underneath it the picture of a seedling that had sprouted and was growing upward toward the ground.

Cynthia did not leave with the rest of them, but spent a long time praying on her knees. She was the one who had asked the presbyters to paint the image of a wheat field on her gravesite, since for her and many others Scintilla was truly the *grain of wheat* of which the Master spoke: she had produced so much fruit. She whom her snobbish countrymen would call a "barbarian," because she came from Gaul! How much she owed to her: *she* who had embraced her on Vatican Hill that painful day after her father had died, when she had felt completely alone in the world; *she* who had patiently taught her about the Master and his Way, especially about how to forgive, and how to deal with Claudia; *she* who had taught Junia and dozens more in Rome, with her charming Gallic accent.

Cynthia was sure that Scintilla was with the Lord, but she could not hold back her tears, which began to flow freely down her face. At that very moment she decided to renew her complete dedication to the Lord Christ, her *Kúrios*. Her life, her whole future, was in his hands. She would gladly volunteer to take Scintilla's place for whatever Pius and the presbyters needed her to do. If that meant serving at tables for the rest of her life, she would gladly do it, though she suspected that the presbyters would ask her to continue teaching the catechumens, and bringing the girls that she tutored to the Lord.

Shortly after his acquittal, Titus made arrangements to sell the house on the Aventine, with the agreement of the men living there. After its sale some of them rented small flats in the city, others returned to live with their families. The biggest problem facing them was where to celebrate the weekly Eucharist. Many decided to go to the Lord's sacrifice at the house of Marius, which was not far from the Aventine Hill.

Titus asked Marcus, who had many connections in the city, to find the best place for Justin to live. He had a Christian friend named Martinus who lived close to the Baths of Timotheus, and who had a fairly large house. Marcus thought that this would be a good place for Justin to stay, since he could give classes to larger groups, and there was room for a few students to live there also. Everyone realized what a great treasure they had in Justin; they planned to introduce their friends to him, and to hear his conferences. As he walked through the streets in his light brown pallium, he was already attracting a lot of attention as an itinerant philosopher.

Marcus also kept speaking with Servianus about the faith, but he could see that his friend was still struggling with certain questions and doubts concerning Jesus.

"I still can't accept the teaching that the Son is equal to the Father," Servianus said. "The idea of the Son being an instrument of the One God, subordinate to Him, seems more in line with Plato's thought. To say that the Son is equal to the Father is to introduce a division in God, and God is One, with no division."

"But that's the big difference between Plato and Christianity, Servianus. Plato had a great mind, but lacked the Son's revelation. It's clear from the earliest witnesses and writings that Jesus Christ was both God and man; he was truly *perfectus Deus, perfectus homo* (perfect God and perfect man). He was not some kind of intermediate being, as Basilides and some of his Gnostic friends are saying."

At that Servianus began to look away from Marcus. It was as if a wall had suddenly appeared between them. "Marcus, I have something difficult to tell you. I hope that it does not hurt our friendship."

"What's that, Servianus? I'm sure it will not . . ." Marcus answered, with a little fearfulness in his voice.

"I've begun to speak with Valentinus and some of his friends. Their ideas are brilliant, and they have a rich symbolism. They have a far more interesting and intellectual view of Jesus and his teachings than other Christians."

Marcus's face fell. He had met Valentinus once in Alexandria. He was a disciple of Basilides, rather more soft-spoken than his mentor but a very effective presenter of ideas, with his own elaborate system of beings and sub-beings coming from God, and with Jesus Christ being only a kind of angel. What's more, he had taught that matter was evil, and even hinted that Jesus was not a real human being, and had not really died on the cross. He heard that Valentinus was in Rome somewhere, but he did not know where. Apparently he was beginning to spread his net of cleverly worded errors, and Servianus was caught in it.

"I have to think, Servianus, and pray. I can't stop you from hearing these speakers, obviously. But would you do me the favor of reading a few things first, and then we can talk about them?"

"Of course, Marcus."

So Marcus gave him a scroll of John's Gospel and two letters of Paul. He also would get one of Justin's works on Plato, though he hesitated a bit since some of Justin's own words about the Logos seemed ambiguous to him at times. After shaking hands they parted for the day. Marcus resolved to pray more for Servianus that week, and to offer his Wednesday and Friday fast for him, in union with the Lord Christ on the cross. He did not doubt Servianus's sincere friendship; after all, he was the one who had alerted him to his father's plot against him. But he was deeply concerned, and even felt personally hurt, that his friend was being deceived by Valentinus and Marcion.

GAIUS AND CARMINA

XXI.

Discalus's business was growing. He had sold his previous fish-shop on the Via Biberatica, and had bought a larger store near the Via Sacra. Thanks to Justus's distribution service, he was now able to sell a greater quantity of fish, including a few more exotic ones from the Cantabric Sea, to the north of Spain. He and Silvia, about two years after their marriage, had rented a much larger apartment away from the Subura district, where the tenements were so prone to fire . . . something that had always bothered Discalus since he lost his wife Drusilla.

His son Gaius was now a strapping young man of seventeen, with curly brown hair and gray eyes. He had continued to help his father in the shop over the years, but Discalus could see that he was yearning for something else. Often Gaius would ask him questions about his ancestor who fought under Cincinnatus,[25] in the heroic days of the old Republic.

"Did he fight in the infantry or the cavalry? How old was he when he enlisted? Where were the battles?"

"I really don't know, son; there are so many legends from those ancient times. But I do know that he was one of Cincinnatus's most trusted captains. He died in the battle against the Aequii in the Alban Mountains. And the most exceptional thing is that he was a plebeian, not a Patrician, as Cincinnatus was. After his death, Cincinnatus made

[25] Cincinnatus was a Roman general and dictator who defeated the city's fiercest enemies in 458 B.C. After his victory, not wishing any special honors for himself, he returned to work on his farm. Much of his life is steeped in legend.

him an honorary member of his own clan, that of Quinctius."

Gaius's eyes always gleamed when he heard tales of courage and battles. From the time he was very small Discalus would hoist him to his shoulders so that he could see the men of Hadrian's legions returning from Britain, or going to one of the frontiers along the Danube. He particularly loved to see the Praetorian Guards marching in parade, with high red plumes on their helmets, and their armor gleaming in the sun. Often he would dream of being a soldier himself, fighting for Rome in some distant place. He knew that his father had actually been an army medic for a while, and always remembered how he had cared for Timotheus's wounds after he was stabbed. Before he became a Christian, he learned of the Lord Christ's praise for the Roman centurion in Capernaum, and Peter's conversion of the centurion Cornelius with his whole household. When he heard his school friends on the street mocking Christians as "old women" and "afraid to fight" he could feel his blood boil within him. A boy from the Via Flaminia had once hit him in the face, then taunted him for being a Christian by saying "now turn the other cheek." His fist had quickly found the jaw of his taunter; he knocked him out, though he later decided to say a prayer for him.

But there was another love working in his heart: his love for Carmina. It had grown in a gradual and natural way from the time they were children, when Justus and Constantia would invite his father and him to supper. Gaius had liked Carmina from the start: her quiet way of smiling and helping people, like her mother Consti; her prayerfulness, especially her devotion to Mary the Master's mother; her beautiful voice and skill with the lyre. Though Gaius loved to think of the challenge of battle, Carmina appealed to something gentle and even deeper inside of him, which he knew was from God. That is why he loved her so.

One day, as they walked together in the park near

Hadrian's statue, Gaius decided to bring up with Carmina the ideas that had been absorbing him for a long time.

"I have two things to ask you, Carmina," he began, as he took her hand gently into his own. "First, you know me well, and that I've always wanted to be a soldier from the time I was young."

"Yes," she said, "and I even know that you and Timo liked to play soldiers with wooden swords in the fields behind my father's house."

"How did you know that?" Gaius said, half laughing.

"Oh, I know more about you than you think," she answered, with a mysterious look in her eyes.

"Well," Gaius continued, feeling a little embarrassed, "I would very much like to enlist as a recruit for the Roman army. But I wanted to ask you first about it."

Carmina was disappointed with his question. She had been hoping that he would bring up something else, closer to her own heart, but she was still honored that he had revealed to her what was on his mind. "Oh, Gaius," she answered frankly, "I've heard so many different ideas from those of the Way about the military. Some say it goes against the Master's spirit of forgiveness and charity, but others point to Jesus' admiration for the faith and discipline of the Roman centurion, and the fact that he spoke of wars and generals in his parables about the kingdom of God. I don't know the answer. But do you really think that a follower of Christ can be a soldier? It means killing people, you know."

"That is what a soldier must do, if he's defending Rome."

"But if the Empire is corrupt, should it be defended?"

"I've thought about that. Certainly there are many corrupt things in Rome, but there are also many good things, including a civilization of order and law which is respected around the world."

"I don't know, Gaius," Carmina said at last, as she invited him to sit with her on the bench next to the pond. They said nothing for a while, but then Carmina turned toward him, with an expectant look on her face.

"Is there something else you wanted to talk to me about, Gaius?"

"Yes, and it's really more important than the first thing. And here is the best way that I can explain it." Then without saying another word, he kissed her lightly on the side of her face, and stroked her long brown hair. "I think that God made us for one another, Carmina, and I would like to marry you."

"Well," she said simply. "That's a lot less complicated than the first question, and I've thought about it a thousand times."

"Really?" replied Gaius with a little nervousness. "A thousand times? And what is your decision?"

"My decision is yes, Gaius, a thousand times yes." Then she turned and gave him a kiss, bigger than the one he had given to her.

"But I have one concern on my mind," she continued. "I need to pray about it more, and speak with my father about it."

"What is it? Can't you tell me now?"

"No, but come to our house in two days, and then you can speak to my father about marrying me."

XXII.

Gaius knew that Justus had to sleep in the first morning hours every day, because of his nightly deliveries of fish to Rome. So he waited until the sixth hour of the day, then ran along the Via Portuensis toward Ostia. He had been in training for many hours those days, so he relished the seven-mile run to Justus's house. As he ran, he kept thinking how wonderful Carmina was, and prayed to the angel Raphael that someday she would be his.

Timotheus was sweeping the front of the house when Gaius came up. "May the peace of Christ be with you, Gaius," he said. "And also with you, Timo," Gaius answered as he embraced him, but not too hard since he knew that the wounds in his back still bothered him after all those years. He had made many friends in Rome, but Timotheus always held the first place in his heart because of all their boyhood experiences together.

"I think I know why you came today, son of Discalus," Timo said. "I knew it would happen someday. I have prayed for both you and Carmina, and I'm sure that the Lord Christ has meant you for one another."

They walked together along the side of the house for a while, and Gaius asked if Timo would say a prayer with him for the success of his visit. Then they both knelt down, facing the East, with Timo supporting himself on Gaius's shoulder. They made the sign of the cross on their foreheads, lips, and chests as they prayed that soon Gaius and Carmina would be married.

As Gaius entered the house he found Justus sitting in a small office next to the atrium. Justus would often go there with his wax tablets and stylus, to calculate how many fish he had delivered to Rome, and what profits he had made. He placed a large wax tablet on the wall, giving the approximate location of fishing ships on the Tyrrhenian, Mediterranean, and Cantabric Seas, and when they were expected back in the ports of Ostia and Puteoli. Carmina was sitting right next to him, dressed in a light blue tunic and cape, and a yellow chrysanthemum in her hair. She had learned to work the abacus from her mother, and was quickly adding or subtracting the numbers that her father was giving her. When she saw Gaius, she raised her eyebrows and smiled at him.

"Peace be with you," Gaius said to them. "I didn't mean to disturb you in your work. Is now a good time to speak?"

Justus turned around briefly, also with a broad smile.

"We're just finishing yesterday's count," he said in his deep voice. "Please have a seat."

Gaius sat on a little wooden bench near the door, watching them work, and giving thanks to God for them both ... it was through this family that he and his father had discovered the Christ. At one point little Tertia, who was just learning to walk, toddled in and threw herself over Gaius's knee. She had obviously gotten out of Consti's sight for a moment, and was exploring the house on her own. Gaius lifted her to his lap, and gave her a kiss on her forehead. He then made little motions with his finger to entertain her, so that the others could keep on working. Finally Consti came in.

"So there you are, little *vaga* (wanderer)," she said as she took her into her arms, though the child was protesting a bit.

"Yes, you're right, she is a little wanderer. Maybe she'll end up in Britannia," Gaius joked.

"Or on the Danube," Justus added, as he looked up from his tablets. Then he politely asked everyone to leave except Gaius. As she walked out, Carmina smiled up to Gaius, who looked somewhat nervous, and patted his arm lightly, as if to encourage him. Justus then motioned to him to take the chair where Carmina had been seated, next to him.

"I think I know the purpose of your visit, Gaius," Justus began. "I've seen it brewing for five years, and both you and Carmina are of an age for marriage. When you and your father joined us in the Body of our Lord, it became even clearer to me."

"I don't feel worthy to have her, sir. She is truly wonderful; I've always admired her beauty and charm . . ."

"She gets both from her mother," Justus answered resolutely, as he shifted his big frame on the sturdy wood chair next to the table. "But there's something we need to discuss seriously."

The son of Discalus looked intently at the big man's face;

he had always had a great respect for Justus. As a boy he had actually considered him to be a kind of giant: one of the strongest men in the world. He had listened in awe when Justus spoke of his conversion to Christ after he had fallen in love with Consti. He also knew that each day he had to deal with many tough fishermen, and that each night Justus offered his travel from Ostia to Rome for God and his people. Now, when he said that he wished to discuss something serious with him, Gaius felt a tremor in his heart.

"And what is that, sir?" Gaius answered in a low, slightly hesitating voice.

"I do believe that my daughter loves you sincerely, and will make a good wife for you. But she told me yesterday that she had one fear—that you would become a Roman soldier."

Gaius nodded slowly, as if he had already considered that. But he said nothing.

"I know that your father served in the army as an assistant surgeon, and that one of your ancestors fought under the great Cincinnatus, but Carmina is afraid for you, especially if God should grant you both a child right away. If you were to be killed in battle, or sent away for a long time to one of the frontiers, she would deeply miss you, and so would the child."

Gaius nodded again, this time more gravely, almost sadly. Though he looked outwardly calm, he could feel the force of his two loves struggling inside of him—that of the Roman army and of Carmina. His stepmother Sylvia had warned him ahead of time that he should consider the matter carefully, and pray to God and to his angel before proposing to Carmina, since she knew Carmina and her mother very well. And he had done so.

"I am willing to renounce my plan to be a soldier for Carmina's sake. But I am not sure how I would support her. I have no desire or talent for my father's business."

"Or mine, I suppose?"

"With all respect, sir, I must answer no."

"Yes, I can tell that you're a soldier, deep inside," Justus said as he rose and put a large hand on Gaius's shoulder. "You love the military life, don't you?"

"Ever since I was a boy."

"Well I know that Carmina wants you to be happy; perhaps marriage with her is not for you."

"No, sir," Gaius raised his voice resolutely and stood up. "I know that God wants us for one another. I'll gladly give up my plan for the army, and find some other kind of work . . . if that is what she wishes. I would never want to lose Carmina."

"Perhaps there's a way, Gaius," Justus said, with the tone of voice of one who has thought about something for a while. "As you well know, Rome has an urban cohort under the *praefectus urbi*. [26] Most of its duties are on the street, controlling the crowds, and keeping order in the city. They are not usually called to fight battles on the frontiers, as in Africa or on the Danube. If you served in the cohort, you could still work in the military, but with less danger than a legionary sent to the frontiers."

"And less glory," Gaius said with a little grimace. He was silent for a moment, as he asked the Holy Spirit to enlighten him. Then he said, "You know, I've always dreamed of being in a big battle somewhere, and doing something great for Rome. But I've always known deep in my heart that the greatest battle is to help men change their lives, and convert to Christ. That is the truest glory, isn't it? I could do that among the soldiers of the urban cohort. Peter actually converted two of his guards in this city, as you know. If the cohort is acceptable to you and Carmina, I'll volunteer tomorrow."

After that the two men embraced one another, laughing. Justus seemed to be the happier of the two, since Gaius

[26] The *praefectus urbi* was an appointed position, with duties similar to a present-day chief of police, thus responsible for public order.

could feel his future father-in-law's joy, as if he were being hugged by a bear, almost breaking his back.

XXIII.

The time came for Gaius and Carmina to be wed. They had agreed that he would join the urban cohort, which should bring enough income to support them for their first year of marriage; if needed, Carmina could always work at her father's business for more money. She was very good at keeping accounts, as she was at singing. "Numbers and music go together, you know," Consti had always told her teasingly, whenever Carmina complained about the tedious work of adding and subtracting.

On the day of the wedding, Consti and Sylvia rose very early and put the finishing touches on the special marriage tunic for Carmina . . . the *tunica recta*, with all of its elaborate folds and ruffles. They arranged her long brown hair into six separate tufts, held by ribbons and spearheads, as was the custom for brides in Rome.

At the seventh hour of the day Gaius the bridegroom arrived to Justus's house, accompanied by his father Discalus. Before her entire family, including little Tertia, Gaius took Carmina's right hand into his own, and publicly pledged to be faithful to her.

Shortly afterward the wedding banquet began, which Consti, Sylvia, and Julia from Gladion's household had carefully prepared. It was set up in the house's large atrium. Justus and Sylvia had invited many of their friends, most of them Christians; all agreed that Gaius and Carmina were one of the most handsome couples they had ever seen. Marcus was also there with Atticus; he was glad for the chance to be with the family that his sister had known, and who had been with her on the day of her baptism. "I'm afraid that I'm not as beautiful as Junia," Carmina told Marcus with a self-conscious grin. To which he answered with a little smile, "I'm sure that my sister is very happy for you, Carmina, and that she is asking the Lord Christ to bless your marriage, and to send you wonderful children." And just after he pronounced the words, Marcus said a silent prayer for her and Gaius. "She was so brave, Marcus, and will always be a tremendous example for me," Carmina said, as she touched his hand lightly. Then she went to speak with the other guests, but not without praying for Marcus's perseverance in his own commitment to God. They all knew that Marcus had given up everything, in order to live as Jesus and his apostles did.

After the banquet Gaius returned to the house where they would be living in Rome, a small flat near his father's new shop, where according to custom the bridegroom waited for his bride. At about the tenth hour, after the banquet, Carmina climbed into a large decorative *raeda*, which Justus had rented for the day. She was accompanied by three small children and two of her good friends, both of whom lived in the city near the Via Sacra. One of them was a Christian, and the other was not. At her side on the leather seat she had placed a spindle and distaff, symbols of her authority as the future mistress of Gaius's home.

When they reached the small house near the Via Biberatica, she knocked on the wooden door with lead trimming, smeared it with lard and decorated it with strands of wool. As was the custom, Gaius, who was waiting inside for her, asked for her name, and she replied, "*Ubi Gaius, ibi Gaia.*" [27] When he heard Carmina's voice outside, he smiled because in their case the old standard marriage formula applied literally, since his name was really Gaius. He and Carmina had joked a lot about that in the weeks before the marriage ceremony. Then he opened the door, to the loud cheers and applause of Carmina's companions, including the three children. Gaius walked out of the house to his bride,

---

[27] Literally, "where Gaius is, there is Gaia." Roman women did not have forenames of their own, but took the name of their husbands.

whom he embraced and kissed; then he lifted her up and brought her over the threshold into his house. Everyone cheered even more at that and followed them into the house, where they saw a colorful spread on the table: an ample supply of figs and vintage wine from Southern Gaul, surrounded by bright red and yellow flowers. There was also the scent of Syrian incense, as Gaius paid homage to the *lares* of his family ancestors.

Toward the evening, Bishop Pius arrived with Father Eusebius, and blessed the marriage in the name of Christ, after hearing Gaius and Carmina exchange their vows of love and fidelity. He read a passage from Paul's letter to the Ephesians about marriage as a great sacrament, the *magnum sacramentum*, and briefly preached about the matrimony of Christians as the living image of Christ's own love for his Church. He also prayed that God would bless them with great happiness together, and grant them many children for his honor and glory.

When all the guests had left, before going to bed that night—where they would consummate their love for the first time—Gaius and Carmina placed a little more incense over the simple hearth in the room that served as their kitchen. They both knelt down, facing the East, and Gaius prayed slowly as he took his bride's hand into his own: "O God, let me offer you the prayer of Tobias this night. I take this sister of mine, not with a selfish or lustful heart, but in order to love her for you, and, if such is your will, to bring children into the world for the sake of your kingdom both in heaven and on earth. I ask this through our Lord Jesus Christ your Son, who lives and reigns with you forever and ever. Amen."

TWO MORE WOUNDS

XXIV.

Marcus was becoming more and more concerned about Servianus. Though nothing was said, he began to sense a certain reserve with which his friend was dealing with him. His answers to him were short, and he seemed embarrassed to meet him in the halls of the Athenaeum, where they were both teaching. One day, as they were leaving the lecture hall around the seventh hour, Marcus decided to take a direct approach. He waited for him to leave his lecture room, then went up to him directly and took him by the arm. "Servianus, let's try to resolve this. There is some worm inside of you. We need to talk; I invite you to some good wine at the tavern on the Via Nomentina." Though Servianus tried to make an excuse, it was very lame, and Marcus prevailed. The tavern happened to be the same place where Dédicus and he had first spoken eight years before.

They sat down at one of the tables, and ordered two tall goblets of wine with some fresh bread and figs. Servianus seemed nervous about the whole encounter, and began to shift his slight body uneasily on the wooden bench.

"Now tell me honestly, Servi, what's the matter? Why are you acting so nervously with me? We used to be best friends."

"I'll be honest with you, Marcus. As I told you before, I've been hearing lectures from both Valentinus and Marcion. I've also talked with them personally. I knew that you wouldn't approve, and I didn't want to offend you. But I find them fascinating in their ideas about God and the Christ."

"But tell me, Servianus, what do you find fascinating about them?"

"From what I can see, Valentinus has a deep grasp of Plato's philosophy, and has connected his demiurge with the Christian Logos. He basically says that Christ is the most perfect creature of the One, his most perfect emanation, and that he was sent to the cosmos to redeem man from matter. Our redemption is a liberation from the slavery of matter through the Gnosis that Christ has brought to mankind."

"I know Plato's philosophy, Servianus; I teach it, and I can tell you that Valentinus's theory is only one interpretation of Plato's demiurge, and pretty speculative at that. His biggest mistake is to connect the demiurge with the Christian Logos, and to make him a creature of the Father only. Christians have always held that the Logos is also divine, and truly the Son of God. Valentinus should not call himself a Christian; he's deceiving many people."

"But what about Marcion, Marcus? His father was a bishop, the bishop of Sinope." [28]

"Yes, Servi, and I've heard that his own father actually excommunicated him for his ideas."

"But why, Marcus? He's studied the Hebrew Scriptures thoroughly and has concluded that the Hebrew God is really evil since he created the world of matter and corruptibility. Valentinus says much the same."

Marcus was getting impatient. He could feel the blood rising to his temples, and his heart began to pound. "But don't you see, Servi, that this is a direct contradiction to the Hebrew Scripture itself, which the Christians consider to be inspired? The very first chapter of Genesis states that God created everything good, even very good. He is not an evil God, but a very good God; matter and the world are not evil."

"But even granting you, for the sake of argument, Marcus, that matter is good, why would the Son of God subject himself to matter, which is so corruptible? Isn't this opposed

[28] Sinope is a port town on the Black Sea, in Asia Minor.

to his divinity, the very divinity that you speak about? Why would an incorruptible God humiliate himself so?"

Marcus reflected a bit, and said a little prayer to the Holy Spirit for inspiration.

"I asked my sister that same question about ten years ago, just after she became a Christian. Why would he become weak and vulnerable—I asked her in order to test her—why did he die on the cross, while still being God? Do you know her answer, Servianus? She simply said that it was because he *loved* us. Then she smiled and did a little dance; I shall always remember that," Marcus said slowly.

Servianus saw how deeply his friend was moved. He didn't want to offend him, or his sister, especially considering how his own family had betrayed Junia. "Perhaps we had better stop discussing this for now," he said, as he smiled at his friend across the table.

"That's all right, Servi. I'm sure that Junia would want us to keep discussing it," Marcus answered. "Keep in mind that we believe that Jesus Christ was truly God and truly man. I'm sure you will agree that it is within God's power to become a human being; this is not opposed to reason. We believe that Jesus Christ was not some kind of apparition or *aeon*, but a man who could feel hunger and thirst, who could shed tears, and feel joys and sorrows, just as you and I do. And unlike what Valentinus says, he had a real body that could suffer and even die on a cross. That is precisely how we believe that he redeemed us, not from some mystical 'Gnosis' or some complicated new revelation."

"But Valentinus says that the beliefs you just gave are for common men who are not enlightened. It is carnal men that hold that Jesus had a real body; the truly spiritual men are liberated by Jesus' ideas and revelation, not by any bodily action. Don't you see, Marcus, how his idea is much more appealing to educated people who know philosophy and can think for themselves?"

"I would rather say, Servianus, that his ideas appeal to

superficial people who don't really want to change their behavior, or do anything that demands real sacrifice."

"But they do require bodily sacrifice, Marcus. Look at Marcion for instance. In his view of Christianity only celibates, or widows and widowers who have not remarried, can be baptized. He is far more demanding than the Catholic Church. He has also rejected many of the Catholic Scriptures as misleading."

"But don't you see, Servianus," Marcus was becoming passionate again, "that his practices are totally against the true Gospel of Christ? Christ said, 'Go and baptize all nations and peoples, in the name of the Father, and of the Son, and of the Holy Spirit.' He never made any distinction between those who are married or not. God wants every individual to be saved, as Paul the Apostle stated in one of his letters. The only distinction that Jesus ever made concerning Baptism was between those who believed and those who did not believe in him."

Servianus shook his head sadly. "It's very confusing to me, Marcus. Can there be two Christs, instead of one?"

"There was and is only one Christ, Servi, but men's pride and stupidity are dividing him."

"Men's pride, or the evil one . . ." Servianus said gravely, and Marcus could only nod his head in agreement.

Marcus and Servianus parted ways after their conversation. The son of Gaius walked home feeling depressed. *The next thing to happen is that these Gnostics will be writing their own gospels, and trying to pawn them off as the real ones, as Basilides has already done in Alexandria.* He said a prayer for his friend Servianus, and vowed that he would always remain his friend, no matter what happened.

Within a month, Pope Pius issued a decree of excommunication against Marcion and his followers, at which point the wealthy shipbuilder from Sinope formed his own Church in Rome, which immediately gained hundreds of followers. Marcus kept trying to see Servianus to speak with him about it, but the son of Antonius kept his distance from him.

XXV.

A few months after his talk with Servianus, Marcus was returning from his morning lectures at the Athenaeum, in order to do his midday prayer. As he approached his small house, he was surprised to see a light-blue litter borne by four slaves, with his mother inside. He went up to it immediately, took his mother's extended hand, and looked up at her face: "What a pleasant surprise, mother," he said, but he could see that she looked troubled and strained about something.

"Can we go into your house, and speak?" Aurelia asked her son anxiously.

The slaves lowered the litter to street level, and Marcus helped his mother to step out of it, drawing aside the curtains for her. He opened the door to the little house and brought her to the room which served for dining and visiting at the same time. He pointed to a small couch in the corner, more comfortable than the two wooden stools that Marcus normally used for himself. After giving him a kiss, his mother went directly to the point.

"I'm very worried about your father, Marcus. He has not been himself of late. Normally he's quite calm, but recently he's been returning from the Senate nervous and muttering to himself. He hardly says a word to me now, though for a time it had been better between us."

As she spoke, Marcus noted worry lines along her forehead, which he had not seen before; there were many gray hairs now showing along both sides of her head.

"One time Marcus," Aurelia went on, in a very low voice, shaking a bit, "I even saw him take a dagger in his hand . . . you know, the one he always kept on the shelf in his study next to the atrium . . . as if he were pondering something

He even made the brief motion of pointing it toward his heart. I saw it from the door, and was about to cry out, but he quickly put it back on the shelf."

Marcus's eyes narrowed and he shook his head slowly, as if trying to understand something. He knew that in the past some Roman Stoics had actually taken their life in moments of great danger or humiliation . . . the most famous being Marcus Portius Cato, who stabbed himself to death rather than to be taken prisoner by Julius Caesar.[29] Afterward many of his countrymen even considered Cato's action to be noble, since in this way he did not have to lose his dignity or self-possession in the hands of his enemy. When he became a Christian, Marcus understood how wrong that action was.

"But why, mother?" Marcus asked anxiously. "Isn't he doing well in the Senate? Isn't Antoninus pleased with his work?"

"It isn't that, son," Aurelia said slowly. "Keep in mind that Junia's death was a terrible blow to him, from which he never really recovered. He loved her so much, Marcus, more than me. A great part of his life died when she died; his Stoicism just could not get him beyond that great sorrow. But now there's something else deeply troubling him . . ." Her voice hesitated, and she looked away from her son for a moment, at the floor.

"Is it I, mother, who am causing him such torment?" Marcus asked in a very low voice.

"I'm afraid so, Marcus. Your becoming a Christian was like a dagger in his heart. He doesn't talk about it much, but it is constantly eating at him inside. He doesn't want to give in to those thoughts, I know, because he's a Stoic, but they keep obsessing and depressing him all the time. I can't get him to relax and think of other things. Oh, Marcus," she raised her voice suddenly, "I'm so afraid that he will harm himself!"

[29] This occurred in the city of Utica (in present-day Tunisia), in the year 46 B.C.

"I must go see him right away," Marcus answered, though feeling very confused, and not knowing what he could ever say to his father.

"It won't work, Marcus," his mother answered. "The only thing that will work is for you to renounce your superstition and then go to see him. Tell him that you are also ready to marry the woman that he wants you to have, to give him an heir . . ."

Marcus said nothing for a while. He felt that he was being hit by an earthquake, and began to feel frightened, for the first time in several years.

"Pray to the gods for me, mother," was all that he could say.

XXVI.

Marcus spent the next few days in agony; he couldn't sleep. He recognized how much he owed to his father, who had given him such good care and moral training as he was growing up. It had always been hard for him, though, to feel the love of a son for him; with his Stoic ideals, Gaius seemed more like some perfect unattainable statue, such as one could see near the Temple of Jupiter on the Capitoline Hill. When he became a Christian, Marcus had tried hard to understand and love his father, trying to countermand his own feelings about him. He certainly did not want his father to give in to bitterness and despair, much less to harm himself on his account. He didn't know what to do. He knew that he could never renounce Jesus and his Way, as his mother wanted; in the past six years it had become his very life, the purpose of his existence. But at the same time, didn't God himself command that one should honor his father and mother? Shouldn't he do all in his power to keep his father from harming himself?

It was the same problem that he had faced on embarking for Alexandria seven years earlier. A subtle little voice inside was beginning to torment him: perhaps he was being selfish by remaining a Christian, and by remaining continent.

He resolved to eat only one meal a day for the week ahead, and ask the Holy Spirit, the Spirit of Truth, to enlighten him. His prayer took on many forms, some times a longer dialogue, other times a quick aspiration. But it was always with a feeling of urgency. *Come, Holy Paracleítos, you who were sent by the Lord Christ to his disciples, you who can penetrate even the deepest corners of my soul, give me the answer . . . and please keep my father from harming himself.*

He also spoke to Father Atticus. Of all the men he had known at the Aventine House, excepting Numer, Atticus was the one he valued the most. Marcus loved talking with him. Though not a philosopher, the young priest had a simple, common-sense view of life, combined with a great love for the Master.

"If he won't see you, why not send him a letter?" Atticus asked.

"But what can I tell him about myself and my commitment that he doesn't know? How can I give him hope for what is really troubling him?"

"Talk to him about the Christian Logos and the great calm and peace that you have found in Christ. Use words that he will understand and appreciate, as a Stoic; you know the Stoic philosophy very well. Let him know how grateful you are for the good upbringing and training that he gave to you and Junia. Above all, be sure to let him know that you are very happy as a Christian. I think that all good fathers and mothers want their children to be happy."

"But what about his desire to have a grandson?"

"Has he ever considered adopting a son?" Atticus asked.

"I'm sure that he has, but I'll put that in the letter also."

After Atticus assured him of his prayers, particularly at the Eucharist, Marcus resolved to follow his advice. After another day of thought, prayer, and fasting, he sat down to write his father in the early afternoon. He had just taken up a papyrus scroll at his desk when he heard an insistent banging at his door. It was the slave Syphon, quite out of breath, who had run all the way from Gaius's house on the Esquiline.

"It's your father, Marcus. He collapsed in his study one hour ago. He's unconscious, and there seems to be little hope for his life. The doctor is with him now."

Marcus crumbled the papyrus scroll in his hand, and rushed out of the house. He ran faster than the elderly slave and reached the beautiful white stone and marble mansion on the Esquiline Hill, where he and Junia had grown up. He entered the atrium, and ran through the crowds of Gaius's *clientes,* who were speaking in hushed tones among themselves but fell silent when they saw Marcus. Then he walked into his father's room. They had placed him on a long couch in the part of the room closest to the courtyard, so that he could get more air. It seemed that he had suffered either a stroke or a heart attack. Aurelia was sitting next to him, fondling locks of her husband's black and gray hair, and holding his hand. When she saw Marcus enter the room, she tried to smile at him, but shook her head sadly at the same time.

"*Domine Iesu, miserere mei,*"[30] Marcus said under his breath as he walked quickly to his father and mother.

He went to the other side of the couch and took his father's hand, calling out loudly and identifying himself: "Father, wake up and look at me; it's your son Marcus!" To everyone's surprise, Gaius opened his eyes immediately and recognized him. He looked at him severely at first, but then his face muscles relaxed, and Marcus could see the hint of a smile in his eyes. He lifted his hands and arms, as if to send everybody away except Marcus—including his wife. Obediently they all left the father and son alone together in the room, and went out to the courtyard, whispering nervously to one another.

[30] Literally, "Lord Jesus, have mercy on me."

"Father," Marcus began in a very unsteady and hoarse voice, "I'm so sorry. I was trying to write . . ."

But Gaius motioned for him to put his ear near his lips. As Marcus bent over him, he could feel his father shaking and trying to summon all of his strength to say something to him. He heard many sounds, but all he could distinguish was the word "God," which he said several times between gasps. After that, Gaius fell into a coma, from which he never recovered. Marcus remained at his side continually, holding his father's hand, and praying to the Lord Christ for him. Within a day, Gaius was dead.

XXVII.

Gaius Metellus Cimber had told his wife many times that he wanted only a simple funeral remembrance, in accord with his Stoic principles. The only reflection or speech at the event was to be given by his good friend and fellow Stoic Ennius, who had also served with him for many years in the Senate. And so it was. After his body had been cremated and the ashes placed in an urn next to the remains of Tullius his father, Ennius proceeded to read a long passage from Epictetus.[31] Then very briefly, and with little emotion, he summarized his acquaintance with Gaius to the hundred or so people gathered in the family atrium. Marcus attended the service with his friends Titus and Philius; he was deeply disappointed, even angered, that Ennius had not mentioned any of his father's accomplishments in the Senate, or his services to Rome and the current Emperor, which were many. But then again, Marcus knew that his father had wanted his funeral to be this way, and Ennius had respected that wish. In thinking about it later, which he often did, he began to admire his father more. He had been true to his

---

[31] First-century Stoic philosopher whose writings provided inspiration for many Greeks and Romans, including Marcus Aurelius, Emperor of Rome after Antoninus.

Stoic philosophy until the end: real virtue should be a reward in itself, and should not be motivated by men's praise and honor.

After the funeral service, Aurelia gave Marcus some news about his father's will that he had hardly suspected. Not only had his father *not* disowned him, but he had left him several hundred thousand sesterces. The fine house on the Esquiline, the country villa, and the servants he had left to Aurelia. Marcus told his mother that he didn't need all that money, and would put it in a fund to help the poor. She couldn't understand why he would do that, and asked him to reconsider—but in the end she left him free in his decision, as her husband had indicated in the will.

After it was all over, Marcus could only give thanks to God for the great favor he had received, and he resolved to pray harder for his father's soul.

THE EMPEROR'S MARCH

XXVIII.

The other Gaius, son of Discalus, was proving to be a very able soldier of the urban cohort. He learned very quickly how to subdue a man, and throw him to the ground; above all, he learned how to use the broad sword, which many Roman soldiers carried at their sides. Though most of his training was in crowd control, he also learned combat skills for the battlefield, in case he was ever called to serve at the frontier, or other troublesome places of the Empire.

There was one other Christian, from what he could see, in the cohort; he was named Varistus and came from Northern Italy, close to the Alps. His family had moved to Rome when he was a boy, and they had all converted to the Church from the preaching of a prophet [32] who had come to the city at the beginning of Hadrian's reign. He had spoken to them of the end times and the coming of Christ, and this, along with the encouragement of some Christian couples that his father and mother had always admired, had brought the whole family into the Church.

It was Varistus who introduced Gaius to Séptimus, captain of the charioteers in the Praetorian Guard. Gaius had heard of Séptimus earlier from Carmina; it was he who had brought Father Atticus so quickly to her little sister, in time for him to give her the sacrament of Confirmation. Though soldiers of the cohort shared quarters with some Praetorians,

---

[32] In the early Church the prophets were inspired individuals considered to be direct messengers of God's word. Many of them went from city to city, and were revered as successors of the Old Testament prophets, particularly of Saint John the Baptist. See Acts 2:17, which speaks of both men and women prophets.

he had never met Séptimus, and thought that he, being a member of the Emperor's elite corps, might be distant or arrogant with him.

It was just the opposite. A slender man, with keen eyes and strong arms, Séptimus was friendly and open with him from the beginning. He remembered Justus and his children, Timotheus and Carmina, and had actually partaken of the Eucharist a few times in their house, especially after little Maria Rosa went back to God. He had also heard of Gaius's prowess on the training field: apparently no other guard of the urban cohort could bring him to the ground, or beat him in a sword fight.

"Gaius," Séptimus told him one day as they were leaving the barracks, "I'm praying for a few soldiers of the Praetorian Guard, so that they find Christ, including Quintus himself. Will you pray for them also?" Gaius was just leaving for duty to a street near the new forum, where two senators were about to make speeches to the people; he had been called with twenty others to maintain order.

"Gladly," said Gaius, "as long as you pray for a few of my comrades in the cohort."

"Agreed," replied Séptimus, and with a hearty laugh they exchanged names, then went their separate ways.

XXIX.

The God of Heaven blessed Gaius and Carmina with a baby boy, within ten months after their union: a stout little fellow, with a good pair of lungs and brown hair like his mother. They decided to name him Discalus after his grandfather. Pius himself baptized him, with his assistant Eusebius. Within eight months Carmina was pregnant again, and was suffering from morning sickness.

One day, when his wife was particularly ill, Gaius was hesitant about going to the cohort, and was thinking of asking for a day of leave. Carmina insisted that he go anyway, but only that he should say a prayer to Mary for her. That day there were many extra drills to go through, in conjunction with the Praetorian Guard, because the Emperor was about to march through Rome, thereby heightening security needs for all the streets. By evening the men were quite tired, and invited Gaius to some wine at a nearby tavern, a favorite resting place for the urban guard. Gaius, who had made some good friends among them, agreed, though he didn't send word to Carmina that he would be late.

When he came home two hours after sunset, not inebriated but a little unsteady, Carmina felt quite angry. She had had a splitting headache for many hours. Little Discalus had been crying all day and had not taken his nap. She had sung all of the lullabies she knew to him, in her softest voice, including the one about "Romulus and Remus"[33] which her mother had sung to her, but to no avail. She had been waiting for two hours for Gaius to come for supper, and he hadn't come. She was beginning to worry. Had he been hurt in training? Why was there no messenger? All kinds of fearful scenarios had flashed through her mind.

"Why didn't you tell me that you would be late, Gaius?" she raised her voice at him as he entered the room. "Your son has been crying all day, and I have had nobody to help me."

Gaius felt like snapping back at her. After all, he did offer to stay at home that day, but she told him to go to work. What's more, he thought defensively, why can't a man go out with his friends some times? Does he have to consult everything? But he decided to say nothing. He managed to subdue his feelings at the moment, and forced himself to give her a smile. He then leaned down and took the child from her lap. The baby stopped crying immediately, as he put his tiny hand on his father's shoulder and gave a contented little sound.

---

[33] The legendary founders of Rome, who were said to have been nursed as infants by a she-wolf.

Carmina said a word under her breath, then shook her head with a kind of helpless frustration. She looked down at the floor, and began to cry softly. "Oh, please forgive me, Gaius, I just feel so poor and wretched sometimes."

"No, Carmina," her husband answered, "you must forgive me. I should have told you that I would be late. I was not being thoughtful of you . . ." Then he bent over and kissed her gently on the forehead, giving little Discalus back to her, who was very peaceful now and went right to sleep after she put him to bed.

As a couple, Gaius and Carmina had the custom of always praying together at the end of the day, no matter how tired they were. But that night, before going to bed, they prayed especially to the angel of their small home, to protect their love for one another, and their two children.

XXX.

Quintus, now Prefect of the Praetorian Guard and married to Claudia, liked Séptimus a lot. He was always reliable, and the best charioteer and horse trainer in the guard. He knew that Séptimus was a Christian: there had already been two accusations on that account against him by other members of the Guard, but Quintus had not forwarded them to the Emperor's court. He knew that they came from jealousy or ambition, since many other Praetorians wanted his job.

Once in a while he would even invite Séptimus to supper at his large home on the Esquiline Hill, with himself and Claudia. He had two slaves from Dacia, who were excellent cooks.

Claudia was polite to Séptimus when he came, but she was suspicious of him since she knew he was a Christian. Her feelings toward Christians had softened after knowing Cynthia, but she was still very opposed to them, as were most people of her class. She didn't want her husband to come close to them in any way. Toward the end of the meal, as they were reclining at the triclinium and the slaves were bringing sweet fruits for dessert, Quintus asked Séptimus about his family.

He said that he had a wife and three children.

"Three children!" Claudia cried out. "How can your wife take it? You should give her a rest, don't you think?"

Quintus shifted uneasily on his couch, setting down his goblet of wine on the low table. Besides the rudeness of his wife's remark, the whole topic of children had been a very sensitive topic between them. In their eight years of marriage they had had only one child, a son who died in childbirth. The entire event was so hard on Claudia that she had not wanted to have another child since then. But Quintus very much wanted to have children, especially a son; he kept bringing up the topic with Claudia, but she never gave him a clear answer. He suspected that his wife might be taking something to prevent having children, though he didn't want to ask her.

He was about to say something to reprimand his wife for her remark and defend his friend, when Séptimus himself spoke up.

"My wife and I both agreed, even before we were married, to have as many children as God wanted to send us. None of my wife's pregnancies have been easy, but we have always considered each child to be a gift from heaven."

"But did she ever lose a child?" Claudia asked rather bluntly. It was clear from the tone of her voice that the whole topic was painful for her.

"Yes," Séptimus answered in a low, very calm voice. "We have lost two, but we are convinced that God did not lose them."

At that, Claudia remained thoughtful for the rest of the meal, and said very little.

XXXI.

The next day Emperor Antoninus was to enter Rome. He planned to form an imperial procession preceded by his Praetorian Guard, going through the Triumphal Arch built by Titus seventy years earlier. Some of the army veterans grumbled about the Emperor taking that route, because, unlike his two predecessors, he had not won any battles in the field. But they said nothing more, since they knew that nobody could oppose the will of Caesar and hope to win.

That day, because of the need for increased security, Gaius was assigned to stay close to the Praetorian Guard, which was marching directly in front of the Emperor's chariot. As one of the most alert and well-trained members of the urban cohort, he was chosen for that duty. It was a clear September day. The sun's rays shone brightly on the Praetorians' armor, and on the bronze of their plumed helmets; a light breeze was rustling through their red cloaks.

Gaius, who had been trained to keep a close eye on the crowds during any public event, noticed a man in a soiled green tunic looking intently at Quintus, who was marching at the head of the Praetorian Guard. There were six or seven men next to him who were not cheering with the crowds, and seemed nervous about something; they were staring directly at the center of the guard line and at Quintus as he marched. Suddenly, as if on cue, all seven of them rushed from the crowd and charged into the center of the guard, which was only two men deep because of the narrow street. One of them was cut down immediately by a guard, but the others managed to stab two other guards, and were converging on Quintus from behind. Gaius tried to draw his broad sword to bring them down but the crowds were so close to him that he could not draw it. Leaping through the people he managed to knock one of the assailants to the ground. He then grabbed the hand of another who was about to stab Quintus in the back of the neck, and deflected his knife. He wrestled the man to the ground, but his knife pierced Gaius's left shoulder. The other soldiers of the guard, now fully alert to the danger, came to his aid and promptly killed Quintus's attackers.

Gaius was slowly rising from the ground, as Quintus turned to look at the man who had saved his life. He was bleeding and holding his left shoulder, but managed to lift his right arm to salute him.

"Well done, soldier, you have saved my life. Please tell me your name."

"I am Gaius, son of Discalus, sir."

"And of what clan, or family name?"

"From the clan of Quinctius, though we are plebeians," Gaius answered proudly, repeating the words that his father had always taught him.

"From the clan of Cincinnatus himself! Then I am not surprised," Quintus answered, with an admiring gleam in his eye. He then asked that Gaius be cared for immediately by his own physician, the best one in the Guard. He himself had not been hurt in the fight, and only later did he learn that the man who saved him was a friend of Séptimus, and a Christian.

ATTICUS

XXXII.

Marcus missed the animated gatherings at the Aventine House, and the chance to meet regularly with a group of Christian men like himself. Once or twice a week he got together with Titus, who now lived with his family, or Philius, who had rented a small house near the Via Sacra; but despite their joking and stories, they could never quite reproduce the warm and joyful atmosphere of the *Domus Aventina* (Aventine House). Titus often apologized, with deep regret, to the other two for his part in having it closed down; it was something he would never forget, and it still haunted him. At first he didn't want to meet with his old friends, out of shame, but Marcus and Philius encouraged him. "Sooner or later, the house on the Aventine would have to be closed, Titus; it was known as a Christian gathering place," Philius said, and Titus knew that he was right. Occasionally Marcus went to Justin's house near the Baths of Timotheus, but the atmosphere there was more like a school or academy for Christian studies; it did not have the home-like atmosphere of the Aventine House.

In the days after his father's death, Marcus had seriously considered becoming a deacon or a priest. He knew that he had the philosophical and spiritual training to become one, and Atticus had encouraged him to do so. But he could never forget his conversations with Numer, who had so inspired him about being the salt and light of the world. The Master himself had spoken in those terms, and most of his parables were about ordinary life and labors. It was obvious to him that Christ's followers did not have to change their condition of life in order to do his will. Most of them were married, but some, like Justin, Numer, and himself had chosen the path of celibacy without being ordained. At times Marcus dreamed of beginning his own philosophy school in Rome, *as a good competition to Justin's school*, he jokingly thought to himself.

Though Marcus did not think that he was called to be a presbyter, Atticus remained his best friend. He would speak with him openly about his family situation, about the classes he was giving at the Athenaeum, even about different temptations and trials he was facing. He loved to go for walks with him at one of the open parks of the city, and once in a while they would go horseback riding in the countryside past the Via Flaminia. Atticus was also an expert horseback rider, having learned about horses on the farm in Gaul where he was raised.

One afternoon, at an hour that they had agreed upon, Marcus brought two riding horses to the place where they usually met. But Atticus did not come, which was completely unlike him. At first Marcus thought that he was taking care of a dying person, or that Pope Pius had given him a last-minute assignment. So Marcus rode for a while alone, then returned the horses to the stable near the Campus Martius. He walked back to Atticus's tenement, but found it empty. Eusebius was not there either. He felt uneasy about the situation, but realized there was nothing else he could do, so he decided simply to return to his house. As he approached it, he saw Titus waiting for him in front of his door with a worried expression on his face. He immediately ran up to him.

"The Lord's peace be with you, Titus," Marcus whispered to him.

"And with you, Marcus," Titus answered, then said quickly, "Have you heard the news?"

"No," Marcus answered, expecting something serious, from the look on his friend's face.

"They've arrested Atticus on the charge of being a Christian priest."

Marcus felt his heart skip a beat, but remained silent.

"We don't know yet who has denounced him, but I have heard that there are two or three witnesses."

"There were three witnesses against you, Titus, but we managed to escape sentencing."

"Yes, but I'm afraid that this time is different, Marcus."

"In what way?"

"In my case the evidence was circumstantial, but the witnesses against Atticus actually claim to have seen him celebrating the Eucharist in a home. And they're all Roman citizens, so they can testify in court."

"They must be false brethren, then," Marcus said sadly. "We have to identify and expel them right away from the assembly."

"Yes, we do, but I'm afraid it's too late for Atticus."

XXXIII.

It was as Titus predicted. Both he and Marcus attended the trial, and the evidence for Atticus's being a Christian priest was very clear. On different occasions all three witnesses— one was a man that Marcus had thought was a catechumen, but he could not identify—had seen Atticus actually celebrating the Eucharistic service, and distributing bread and wine to those of the fanatical sect. The law was clear, and sentence was passed very quickly. It did not help matters that Atticus was not a Roman citizen, though he had worked as an architectural aide for Turibius. If he did not offer wine and incense to the Roman gods, and renounce his belief in Christ, he would be sent *Ad Metalla*, to the mines.

Marcus shuddered when he heard that phrase. Everyone knew that the mines were the worst place on earth to send anyone. The food was contaminated, the guards were particularly brutal, and there was hardly any air to breathe, with the prisoners packed together like animals. A healthy man or woman might survive a year or two, but there would always be fresh replacements to bring the Romans their lead, silver, or gold. One of the biggest mines was in Dacia,[34] where Atticus might be sent.

Marcus's priest friend was put in a cell that smelled heavily of human excrement, at the deepest level of the Mammertine Prison, where Peter and Paul had been jailed, and most recently Pope Telesphorus. He was allowed only two visitors: Eusebius, who came to hear his confession, and give him the Pope's blessing, and Marcus. Marcus was overwhelmed by the stench, as he walked down the steep stairs; when he entered the narrow prison, he looked very pale, and his hands were shaking.

"Oh, Marcus," Atticus said with a little smile, "it looks like you are the one condemned."

"I can't help it, Atticus, I fear very much for you; and even more, I fear for myself, because I am losing you, the one who taught me most about the Christ."

"Numer also did," Atticus corrected him.

"Yes, but you taught me about his life and gave me his sacraments. Oh, Atticus . . . I'm going to miss you tremendously," Marcus cried out as he embraced his friend, his body trembling with emotion.

"Marcus," Atticus answered in a hoarse voice, trying to hold back tears, "it's whatever God wants. Remember that the Christ predicted that this would happen. I actually feel privileged to be one of his witnesses now."

"Yes, Atticus, but the mines are a living death. At least my sister had the consolation of having everything finished with the stroke of an axe, and those who are burned or thrown to the lions also end their lives quickly, but your punishment is a slow and tortuous hell."

---

[34] The Romans operated a large gold mine in this country (present-day Romania).

"God will give me strength, Marcus, but please pray for me . . ."

Within two days, along with many other prisoners condemned to the mines, Atticus was forced to walk the fifteen miles between the city and the port of Ostia on the Tyrrhenian Sea. Along the road were lines of people watching the condemned men and women, who had iron rings around their necks, and were chained to one another. Some of them were fathers and mothers of children. Those condemned had been branded on the left side of their faces with a red-hot searing iron, and their deep scars were still filled with blood and pus. Some of the onlookers were silent, some looked away with a mixture of horror and pity, some yelled out curses: "Criminals!" "Enemies of the Emperor!" "Dirty Christians!" "You deserve it!"

But there were some persons in the crowds who had different thoughts, and were praying for Father Atticus and those condemned with him. Four presbyters, including his roommate Eusebius, were looking at him with both hope and admiration in their eyes. "Thou art a priest forever; may the Lord give you strength," they were whispering softly. One of them, a younger priest, was praying Psalm 23 for him: "For the Lord is my shepherd, and though I walk in the shadow of death, I shall fear no evil." It was the same psalm that Atticus himself was saying at that moment. As he passed by Titus and Philius, and a few others who used to live at the Aventine House, Atticus's eyes lit up; he made the V-for-victory sign to them, and gave a blessing, as Pope Telesphorus had done ten years earlier. A little farther down the road he saw Cynthia, Frieda, and Statira, who were actually cheering for him openly, in front of everyone, trying to drown out the insults of those around them. *What courage you have, dear sisters, like Mary his mother*, the young presbyter thought to himself, as he smiled at them and gave them a blessing.

The forced march would make him pass directly in front of Justus's property, and Atticus knew that there also would be Christian faithful waiting and praying for him. As he approached that well-known field with the small vineyard in front, he saw Constantia standing along the road holding little Tertia, who was trying to wiggle her way down to the ground from her arms. Justus and Timotheus, who was leaning on his father's strong shoulder for support, looked at him with a great love and admiration, and waved to him warmly. Gaius, who had requested to be off duty that day, was next to Carmina, now very close to delivering her baby. Atticus gave her a blessing, knowing that it must have been hard for her to come all this way to greet him at her parents' house. He then waved to Gaius and his little son Discalus in his arms. Right behind them stood Gaius's father Discalus, the fish merchant, and his wife Silvia, whose marriage he had blessed.

Suddenly several other persons, men and women, came up to Atticus and began to walk beside him on the road. Some were smiling and singing, while others were looking up to the sky and saying *Maranatha . . . Come, Lord.* The guards menaced them with their spears, trying to force them from the road. At that point one of them, dressed in a perfectly folded toga, told the soldiers to let them alone, since they were members of Atticus's family, and were accompanying him on his last journey. The soldiers, being surprised at the tone of command and authority in the man's voice, then let the people accompany Atticus and keep singing.

The man with the commanding and noble voice was Marcus.

Atticus grinned at his friend when he saw him, though he could not grin much because of the pain of the red burn on his face. Marcus walked in silence with Atticus for all the remaining miles to Ostia, where the ship to Dalmatia was waiting; from there the prisoners were to be taken to Dacia. The other Christians also accompanied them, praying the

Our Father and singing a hymn to Christ the Good Shepherd. As they neared the dock at last Marcus spoke.

"Dear friend, you know that our prayers, our very lives are with you. I would go to the mines myself, instead of you, if I could. Please believe me when I say that . . . ," Marcus added with a faltering voice.

"No Marcus, you must strengthen our community here. Teach the good word, use your philosophy to convert many, with Justin. I'll be praying for you . . ."

They walked a little farther, and seeing how serious and solemn Marcus had become, Atticus said jokingly: "I'll have to enjoy the sun while I can; I hear there's not much of it where I'm going. But I hope to see something better."

"What's that, Atticus?"

"Souls. Think of the other Christians condemned to the mines with me. They'll need encouragement, they'll need prayers, they'll need forgiveness at times. God is sending me to them. Perhaps I can even win over some of those poor prisoners to the Lord Christ . . . they'll have no other hope."

Marcus said nothing after that, but just kept walking and praying for his friend. He felt totally helpless, as if a central part of his life was being taken from him. As they approached the dock at last, Atticus looked at Marcus for the final time, and called his attention to a small cloth bundle that he was carrying at his waist, under his cape. The guards hadn't noticed it, but the young priest's eyes gleamed at his friend when he said: "This is the best of all, Marcus: it's bread and wine."

XXXIV.

Marcus knew that he had taken a big risk by accompanying Atticus in public, but he didn't care. If his time had come to give his life for Christ, so be it. There were no denunciations, however, in the following days, and he continued with his normal teaching schedule at the Athenaeum. With

Atticus's words still ringing in his mind, he began to pray that he could find students who would be open to hearing the message of the Gospel. Somehow there had to be a way.

About a month after Atticus had been sent to the mines, on returning from the Athenaeum, he saw a papyrus with a brown seal hanging from his door. At first he thought that it might be from his mother: he had been visiting her regularly after his father's death. But the scroll looked quite worn and scratched up, as if it had traversed many miles. As he broke the seal and opened it, he saw that it had come all the way from Ephesus, from a person that he had never met whose name was Pyrrho.

He entered his house and read it immediately:

To Marcus Metellus Cimber from Pyrrho and all the breth-
ren at Ephesus.

Greetings in the Lord Jesus Christ, to whom be praise for-
ever and ever, in whom is all consolation and hope. Amen.
Amen.

It is with a heavy but trusting heart that I write to you,
Marcus. Though we have never met, we do have a common
friend named Dédicus of Samaria, whose original name
was Yéshim. He worked with Justin for almost a year in
this city, and has continued here after Justin's departure to
Rome. He has brought many to the Church through his
words, showing how the Lord Christ is truly the fulfillment
of all philosophy, and is in himself the Way, the Truth, and
the Life for every man and woman . . . Jew and Gentile.

As you may know, many of our brethren in this city have
been attacked by anti-Christian mobs on the street, and
have lost their lives . . . including fathers and mothers of
families. Toward the ides of October, Dédicus, on his way to
the house of the catechumen Eugenes, was attacked by a
group of five men. They had cursed at him the previous day
for being a Christian, and Dédicus had simply walked by

them, saying a prayer for them. But the next day, armed with knives and one broad sword, they surrounded him on the street, calling him a criminal and enemy of Diana, goddess of Ephesus. One witness said that Dédicus had tried to defend himself, and knocked two of them to the ground, but there were many men with knives, and shortly after their attack he fell asleep.[35] He was buried in the Lord Christ, at the cemetery just north of the city. A large gathering of his friends and students was there, all praying for his soul. The presbyter Dimitrion led the service.

I particularly wanted to write you, Marcus, since Dédicus so often spoke of you.

He would ask his friends and students to pray for you frequently, as he would turn to the south, toward Jerusalem and his homeland. He called you and Numer his best friends, and spoke often of the work you and Justin were doing in Rome to spread the word of Christ.

May the Lord's peace be with you, Marcus. Please remember us in your prayers and works, as we remember you; we are all united in Christ's sufferings, and in his wounded body. In the words of the Apostle, who spent many days in our city ten decades ago: "Have Christ dwelling through faith in your hearts, being rooted and grounded in love." [36]

Vale. Pyrrho of Ephesus

The letter was beautifully written, but could not take away the intense pain that Marcus felt in his soul after he read it. *First my father, then Atticus, and now Dédicus ... O God, will the crucifixion never end? Lord Christ, give me the strength to endure this!* Marcus tried to hold back his tears. It had been many years since he had cried; the last time was at the tomb of his sister on the night of his Baptism, when Atticus held the lantern for him to read the inscription. But he could not hold back his emotions. He knelt down on the

[35] To "fall asleep" was an early Christian expression meaning to die.
[36] Eph 3:17–18.

floor next to the small stone oven where he prepared his food; streams of tears rolled down his cheeks, and he began to sob uncontrollably. He knew that he should really be giving thanks to the Lord for giving him such crosses, but the whole thing was too overwhelming for him. He felt totally helpless, like a small piece of driftwood tossed about in a stormy sea. He could not figure out anything; he recalled that Dédicus had once told him not to try to do that. There was only pain and sorrow. "*Eli, Eli, lama sabactani,*" [37] he managed to pronounce between his sobs: deep in his heart he knew that he was experiencing just a tiny portion of the Lord's pain on the cross.

---

[37] Aramaic for "My God, my God, why hast thou forsaken me?" (Mt 27: 46).

SATURNALIA

XXXV.

The next day he delivered the news to Titus and Philius, and some of the other fellows who used to live at the Aventine, and knew Dédicus. He gave them a few details about his death, but kept the letter for himself. He knew that shortly they would be receiving the news from other sources, perhaps from letters or travelers to Rome. They all took the news prayerfully and with faith; Philius particularly tried to console and encourage Marcus, for which Marcus was grateful.

The next two weeks were very hard for him, nonetheless. He felt that he was in a kind of daze. It was very hard for him to prepare his classes in philosophy: after all, what could Plato say or do to mend a broken heart? He kept thinking about Dédicus, and was trying to pray to him for hope and strength, since he knew that he was with God. He visited with Titus and Philius, but he continued to be depressed. His mother tried to console him (she had met Dédicus a few times when he was in Rome) but she could not give him what he really needed, since she did not believe in Christ.

He began to feel spiritually weak, and for the first time in many years, doubts about Christ and the Way began to appear in his mind. What if their belief was a massive disillusion, or a kind of wishful thinking? What if Christianity was really only a superstition, as his father once said? Why can't the Christians be like everyone else in the Roman Empire? He fought against those thoughts, but they kept plaguing him with the insinuation that all his efforts were for nothing, and that he and the other Christians were fighting an impossible battle, since the whole world was against them. How easy it would be, he thought to himself, to throw everything away . . .

The Saturnalia festival arrived in Rome.[38] From his little house Marcus could hear the sounds of merry-making outside of his door. There was loud laughing, cursing, and many shouts and screams . . . a mixed cacophony of men's and women's voices. "*Io Saturnalia,*" they were shouting. "*Io Saturnalia!*" Christians generally remained in their homes during the Saturnalia evenings, not only to avoid temptation, but for their own safety and for their children. The first two days of the festival Marcus also stayed inside; on the first night several of his friends had a celebration at Justin's house, where they sang and told funny stories, as a kind of *good* Saturnalia. Marcus had enjoyed it, and it helped him to get rid of some of the grief eating at his soul.

But on the third night he preferred to remain by himself in his house. He did not really have much to do, since there were no lectures to prepare at the Athenaeum, which was closed down for the holidays. He tried to read a few things by the light of his oil lantern, but he began to feel discontented and restless. He attempted to pray, but nothing came to his mind or heart. At last he convinced himself that he needed some kind of escape from his melancholic thoughts. *It wouldn't hurt to take a walk outside*, he told himself, though he didn't feel quite right about it. He put a cape around his shoulders and leather walking shoes on his feet, since it was chilly. But there were so many people in the crowded streets that he hardly noticed the weather. Torches and lanterns lit up the streets, and there were revelers all around him, including many women in loose clothing. As he walked, he remembered that he had committed many sins during this feast before he had met the Lord Christ. It was on the third

---

[38] The games and celebrations between December 17 and 23, in honor of the god Saturn. They were often marked by drunkenness and sexual promiscuity.

night of the feast, precisely this one, when he had met the priestess of Cybele. He had seen her walking in the religious procession with her stylish Phrygian hat, had spoken with her, and then gone into her house later that evening—at her invitation. Would she still be walking in that procession, after so many years? How many lovers had she had? And what about the women near the temple of Isis? He began to feel weak, with the old demons rising inside of him. *Yes, I am a Christian, but what if for just this once . . . ?*

Suddenly he heard shouts and loud screams around him, but it was not "*Io Saturnalia!*" It was "*Cavéte! Cavéte!* Run for your lives!" He looked up the narrow street and saw a huge *raeda* drawn by four mammoth horses careening toward the corner where he was standing. It was being driven by a man who was obviously drunk, perhaps as a joke or as a wild bet with someone. Up the street he could see two bodies—a young man and woman dressed in festive garbs—who had already been trampled by the horses. To his horror he saw a young boy desperately running down the street trying to escape the huge hoofs and wheels. Marcus said a prayer to his angel, and within a second he had run in front of the speeding *raeda* and pulled the boy to the side of the road, a mere instant before it came crashing upon the very place where he and the boy were standing.

The boy, about eight years old, was crying and shaking with terror, and was clinging to Marcus as if he were the only thing in the world that he could trust. Marcus tried to calm him down. About three minutes went by, when a rather disheveled man and woman came up to him. They looked like plebeians and identified themselves as the boy's parents. They said they were taking part in the night's revelry, and had brought their son with him. But Marcus could barely understand them, since their voices were slurred from drinking. They almost seemed amused at what had happened, as if it were part of the night's fun. They didn't even thank Marcus for what he had done. But the boy kept trembling and crying, holding Marcus tightly, and did not run up to the man and woman.

"Shame on you both," Marcus said harshly. "Your son could have been killed."

"All right. All right . . ." the man said angrily, realizing the truth of what Marcus said. "Just give him back."

"I won't give him back until I know that he will be safe."

The man then cursed both the gods and Marcus, and took a swing at him. But the man was so unsteady that the son of Gaius with one motion of his arm brought him crashing to the ground. The woman then began to scream for help, but everyone else was screaming all around them, so it made no difference.

"Listen," Marcus shouted above the din to both of them. "I'm taking the boy to my home for the night." The child was still clinging to him and crying. "If you want him back you can find me on the Via Lupona, in the small red house near Hadrian's Athenaeum."

They both then ran at him, but Marcus shoved them away and took the boy in his arms, heading down the street toward his house. The couple followed him for a while, cursing at him; but then they met another drunken group, laughed, and entered another tavern.

XXXVI.

Marcus put the boy to bed right away, once he got home. His name was Lucius, and his father—the man who had attacked Marcus—was a baker who worked not far from the old forum. He couldn't find out much more, because the boy was exhausted. Marcus gave him something to eat, and Lucius went promptly to sleep.

But Marcus couldn't sleep. He began to recognize that he had just been given a tremendous grace from his Father God. He realized that he had been in a far more dangerous situation than this little boy. He was being severely tempted against chastity and his commitment to Christ, but God had awakened him violently and dramatically. He remembered how he had met Christianity several years before, when Dédicus had saved him in the street, just as he had saved little Lucius. Could it have been Dédicus himself, now a martyr in Christ, who had sent him this grace? He could not stop thinking of the whole event. It was truly a miracle of grace and love, and a mystery at the same time. *No, he mustn't try to figure it out, just as Dédicus once told him . . . he must simply give thanks.* With that he felt a great peace entering his soul, and he went to sleep at last, despite the din in the street.

The next morning, as the sun's rays poured through his small front window, Marcus got up and offered his day to the Lord Christ. He let the boy sleep for several hours after the sun had risen, but finally he heard some stirring in the couch by the door, and a yawning sound. "Good morning," Marcus said with a loud voice and gave him a bright smile. The boy looked up at him shyly, without saying a word, but then smiled back. He seemed very grateful for what Marcus had done. Marcus had some breakfast prepared for himself and the child, and invited him to the table. He was a quiet little fellow with brown eyes and dark hair. As they ate, Marcus asked him several things about his school, games, and friends in the simplest way, but got nothing more that monosyllabic answers.

Finally he asked if he had ever heard anything about the Christians. At that the little fellow's eyes lit up, and he quickly found his tongue. "Oh, the Christians! They're terrible people who are enemies of the Emperor. They won't offer sacrifice to the gods of Rome, and they eat the body and blood of their children at nights!"

Marcus tried not to laugh, as he passed the little fellow a piece of bread and cheese.

"Well that's a very serious matter, Lucius. But tell me, have you ever met a Christian?"

"Well, no. But I've seen them being led through the streets to the Colosseum."

"Did they look very mean to you?"

The little boy suddenly sat up very straight, and scratched his head. It was as if Marcus had asked something that he had never thought about, something very surprising to him.

"No," he said hesitantly in a low voice. "Some of them were actually smiling, and once I heard two of them singing. That's strange, isn't it?"

"Yes," answered Marcus gravely. "I wonder why they were so happy."

"Maybe," the boy offered, "because they're crazy."

"Yes," replied Marcus, "but maybe they believe that they're going to a place of great happiness."

"How can the lions be a place of great happiness?"

"I mean *after* the lions."

The boy simply shook his head in bewilderment.

"Can I go home now?" he asked presently.

"Do you want to go?"

"Oh, yes, my father is a baker and he gives me fresh bread every day with honey."

"Now I know why you want to leave so soon!" Marcus teased. "I only gave you plain bread with cheese . . ."

At that moment they heard two soft raps at the door. Marcus got up from the table and opened it. It was the boy's father, the same one who taken a swing at him the night before. Lucius was delighted and ran to meet him; he had apparently forgotten everything that had happened the night before. Marcus thought that the man must have a splitting headache, but he was well groomed and seemed alert, though his breath still smelled of alcohol.

"My wife and I thank you, sir, for what you did for our boy last night. We should never have taken him with us. I apologize for trying to hit you."

"That's all right. My main concern was for little Lucius. Would you like to come in and visit for a while?"

"Thanking you, sir, but I'll be on my way now. I wish you a good day."

Marcus could tell that this plebeian merchant felt uncomfortable speaking to him, perhaps because of his educated and Patrician way of speech, perhaps because he was still angry for being thrown to the ground.

"Father," little Lucius said as they were about to leave the house, "can I give him a hug?"

"Of course, son, if he doesn't mind."

As Marcus bent down to receive his hug, the eight year old whispered a question in his ear: "Sir, are you a Christian?"

"Maybe so," Marcus answered, with a little gleam in his eye.

As they were leaving he said a prayer to the angels for them both. He had a feeling that someday he would see that little boy again, but he knew not when or where.

THAT ALL MAY BE ONE

XXXVII.

After they had left, Marcus decided to spend the whole day praying and giving thanks for what had just happened to him. He remembered the words of the great Apostle: "For those who love God, all things work together for the good."[39] He reflected on the last twelve years of his life, and how God had truly been with him, beginning with Dédicus's saving him on the street. Now he had saved another human being as well. He had never suffered in his life as much as he had suffered in the past three months, and he had never been tempted so strongly since before he was a Christian . . . yet, somehow through that chance event on the street, God had purified him and lifted him up.

He yearned to receive the Eucharist, his closest contact with Christ each week, but he would have to wait another three days until the Sunday Eucharist at Marius's house. That would be the moment to dedicate himself once again to the Lord Christ, with his precious Body and Blood inside of him. He made an act of contrition for his wavering thoughts and for dialoging with infidelity: he had almost lost his continence, the pearl of great price, for a bowl of lentil soup, as Esau did.[40] He planned to find Father Eusebius as soon as he could, to confess his sin.

It was about the sixth hour that he heard another knock at the door. He was expecting no visitor that day, and thought

---

[39] Rom 8: 28: "for those who love God, all things work together unto good."

[40] See Gen 26: 29–34. Esau, in a moment of weakness, gave up his inheritance as the first-born son of Isaac to his brother, Jacob.

that it could be some confused reveler from the previous night. When he opened the door, he gasped out loud. He could hardly believe his eyes. It was Numer.

"What a shock, Numer!" Marcus cried out. "How did you ever get here? It's winter time . . ."

"Well," his African friend answered, giving him a broad smile with gleaming white teeth in perfect contrast with his ebony complexion, "if you let me in, I'll tell you."

Still hardly believing what he was seeing or hearing, Marcus let him into the room and immediately gave him a huge embrace, so warm and tight that Numer gave out a little cry of pain. To Marcus it was all a dream, a fantastic dream, from what had occurred the night before to this ecstatic moment.

"But how did you get here? None of the ships are at sea at this time of the year," Marcus said, as he fetched a glass of wine and some figs for his friend.

"Oh," Numer said casually, "one of my travel angels just took me over the little puddle from Africa to Europe."

Marcus could only laugh, as he had always done with Numer and his fascinating ways. Seeing him reminded him of the old times at the Aventine House, when Marcus felt perfectly carefree, as if he were sitting on top of the world. He began to feel the burdens and worries of the past month dropping from him, as old leaves drop from a tree when a fresh wind blows. But looking at Numer's face he could see a few lines and wrinkles above his eyes that weren't there before, along with some gray strands mixed into his black curly hair.

"I wanted to come as soon as I could, Marcus. I heard about Atticus's sentence, and that was hard enough, but when I learned of Dédicus's death, I suffered even more. I cried all that night. I knew that you would need some support, so I wanted to visit you as soon as I could—to speak and pray with you."

"I can honestly tell you that Christ has already come to

me, Numer, with a support that you could not imagine."
Then Marcus proceeded to tell him the whole story: about
the Saturnalia, about his wavering faith and strong temptation, and about how it had all ended with his saving of
Lucius from the murderous *raeda* in the street.

"That surely came from God," his African friend responded immediately, in his strong and confident way, which
had always been such an anchor point for Marcus. "And I can
see very clearly our brother Dédicus's strong intercession for
you in that precise moment. He's still very much your friend,
and he's watching over you from Paradise."

The two spent the rest of the day together. There was so
much to talk about that words seemed inadequate to express
all that was in their minds and hearts. Marcus showed him a
tract he was preparing against Valentinus and Marcion. He
was going to review it with Justin after the Saturnalia days
were over. Numer had a few corrections and suggestions, but
basically agreed with it all.

"Where did you learn all those things about the Logos?"
Numer asked him after their session, with a little twinkle in
his eye.

"Why, a short fat fellow from Africa told me about it,"
Marcus quipped back. "But I can still out-wrestle him."

After *prandium* (lunch) they took a walk around the city,
visiting many familiar sites. They walked up the Aventine
to the house filled with so many memories for them both,
now possessed by an olive merchant from Puteoli and his
wife. "It served its purpose for a while," Numer said. "But
you fellows really had to move on, given the situation. I'm
anxious to tell you about the new place that I have started
in Alexandria. You saw the beginnings of it when you were
there."

That night Numer stayed at Marcus's home. The shouts
and noises of the Saturnalia were all around them, but they
didn't affect Marcus now at all. They actually helped him to
speak more about Atticus and Dédicus with his friend, and

to share his dream to bring some fellows at the Athenaeum to Christ.

Numer encouraged him strongly in his plan. "Do you remember that conversation we had once, Marcus? Here we are in the middle of this crazy world, and the Lord is telling us *you are the light of the world, so let your light shine.* Therefore let the light shine, Marcus, let it shine . . . and be the salt in many people's lives. You must be his witness right where you are."

Before retiring that night they prayed the *Nunc Dimittis* of St. Luke's Gospel, standing and facing East, toward Jerusalem. Then Marcus recited a short prayer to Mary Mother of Jesus that Atticus had taught him. Numer slept on the couch in the corner of the room, where the little boy had slept. Despite the noises of revelry outside, despite all the new thoughts and plans that were racing through his mind, Marcus went right to sleep. His last conscious thought was from the great Apostle Paul: "*Diligentibus Deum, omnia in bonum.*"[41]

XXXVIII.

Early the next day Marcus and Numer visited Justin at his large house close to the Baths of Timotheus, on the Viminal Hill. Needless to say the fiery philosopher was overjoyed to meet his old friend and colleague; he too had no idea that he would be coming. Word spread quickly from Justin and Marcus throughout the whole community in Rome that Numer was back. They all gave thanks, remembering how much he and his friends had done to develop the Church in Rome. Many of them, both men and women, planned to celebrate the Sunday Eucharist at Marius's house, which Numer was going to attend. It was rumored that Pius himself would say the Mass.

---

[41] See Rom 8: 28: "for those who love God, all things work together for the good."

On the day before the Mass, however, Titus, Philius, and others prepared a dinner for Numer with a special gathering afterward, as they used to do at the *Domus Aventina*. Justin's atrium was large enough to hold many fellows, including some of the catechumens who were coming closer to Baptism, and who had heard a lot about Numer. Marcus and two others who were good cooks volunteered to prepare the main meal; he included a few Alexandrian dishes that he knew Numer would enjoy. Justin, being the senior of the group and Numer's mentor, presided over the supper and led the prayers. The meal consisted of beef, boiled vegetables and leeks, freshly baked bread, honey, and a vintage wine from Hispania. For dessert there was a large assortment of figs and sweet fruits.

Afterward, as they always had done at the Aventine House, the young men went into the atrium, which had a large red fresco of a stag bounding over a hill. Justin did not have enough chairs for them all—there were about twenty fellows—so most of them sat on their robes or togas, or on small cushions that they brought from the triclinium. It reminded Marcus of that first visit he had made to the Aventine House with Dédicus twelve years before.

Numer, seated in the middle, began the afternoon with an account of the growth of the Church in Alexandria. He had been there for the past ten years, and had seen many changes. More and more families were coming into the Church, including that of the head Roman centurion stationed there. There were many philosophy students interested in Christianity, mostly young men from Ephesus, Antioch, and Jerusalem—though he had recently met one very promising fellow from Cappadocia.[42] Numer explained that he had gotten a teaching post at one of the Platonic academies in Alexandria, and so had been able to meet a lot of young men with inquiring minds.

[42] A Roman province corresponding to the eastern part of present-day Turkey.

"Many simply look at philosophy as a career," he continued, "since Alexandria offers tremendous possibilities in that field, but others are searching for a truth beyond the phenomena of the changing world . . . something to which they can give themselves. Some have strong attractions to Syrian and Egyptian mystery religions, like that of Osiris. But when they hear the real message of Christianity—*that God had actually become a man*—they are astounded. None of those other religions could make such a claim."

At that point Justin intervened in his excited high-pitched voice. "Yes, as I've told you all many times, that was my story as well. I studied many different kinds of philosophies as a young man, and investigated many different religions, until I realized that it was only the Christian Logos which could fulfill, and even supercede, the insights of Parmenides, Plato, and Aristotle. I also discovered that many thoughts of the Hebrew prophets were actually behind those philosophers' systems, though some may not have known it."

"That's right," added Numer warmly, agreeing with his mentor, "and I found that if Christ the Logos is presented as someone who not only creates the existing world, but sustains it with his love and power, students are immediately fascinated. Of course they will always need God's gift of faith to accept Christ personally: we all know that the Savior is more than an idea, but a way of life that demands personal change. That is quite hard for many of them; they have to give up a lot of things that they were doing before."

"Did you ever meet Basilides's disciple Valentinus there? He's in Rome now, you know," Marcus asked, especially thinking of his friend Servianus.

"Yes, I told him to his face many times that he was betraying the foundations of Christian belief, and using Plato to do it. He is making the *pleroma*, or ideal world, something completely separate from the *kenoma*, or real world. He's presenting Christ as a kind of demiurge, who is not divine, and separating God from the real world."

"With the sad consequence," Marcus added, "that he considers matter to be something evil, and that there are really two worlds, one good and one bad. Marcion is teaching the same thing, and has formed his own Church with that belief, as we all know. That directly denies the goodness of creation stated in the book of Genesis."

"As you can see, Numer," Justin said gravely, "we need your prayers for our work here in Rome."

"Gladly," the stout African answered with one of his charming smiles, "but I would also ask your prayers for something."

"What's that?" Justin asked.

"Please pray for Apelles, a student from Cyprus, and his friend Liberianus. They've actually become catechumens in Alexandria, and will be baptized soon. Apelles is seeking to marry, but Liberianus has chosen the path of continence for the sake of Christ's Kingdom."

"Liberianus, you say?" Justin spoke up. "I, too, have a man named Liberianus coming here for instruction; he's to be baptized at the coming Easter Vigil, God willing."

At that, all twenty fellows cheered and applauded, and a few of them joked about the coincidence and the meaning of their names, since Liberianus in Latin means the "one who has been freed."

"Friends," Philius said, "at this point I move we pass to the next part of our gathering. Two of my companions here, Andronicus and Clipeus, were about to fall asleep. The applause has awakened them. I fear that up to this point the wine has been too good, or the philosophical talk has been too deep for them."

That produced a roar of laughter. "Music!" someone shouted. "Jokes!" cried out someone else. "*Io Saturnalia!*" another yelled, though it seemed to be in poor taste. The person who yelled it was the first to perform, as he mounted a little platform in the middle of the atrium. He had actually composed a little poem about the popular pagan festival which began with the refrain: "*Io fatualia, Io ebrialia, Io saturnalia!*" (Hurray for foolishness, Hurray for drunkenness, Hurray for Saturnalia) . . . and the rest of the poem showed in a satirical way how much harm some people can do to themselves while trying to have fun. Titus next told a hilarious story about the great philosopher Thales who kept falling into holes in the ground while looking up at the skies. "With no offense of course to our philosophers Justin, Numer, and Marcus . . ." he added at the end, to general laughter and applause. Another fellow, whom Marcus had not met, then climbed the platform and did some magic tricks; he had actually brought with him a small rabbit, which he kept hidden inside his toga, and which he kept pulling out mysteriously at certain points of his performance.

But the culminating moment of the afternoon's entertainment came with Numer and his legendary flute. They all saw that he had brought it with him, and kept egging him on to play it. Finally he acquiesced. "All right," he said, "I will play it, but only if Proclus accompanies me." Proclus was a husky good-natured man with an aphonic voice, who always produced a laugh when he tried to sing. Marcus recalled that unforgettable afternoon at the Aventine when he and Numer formed a duet: there was no stopping the applause. This time was no different. When Proclus would sing the wrong note, Numer played a wrong note. But when Proclus by chance would sing the right note, Numer played the right note, though once in a while just to tease everyone, Numer would play the wrong note with a little flourish at the end. During the entire performance Proclus would feign indignation, claiming that he was really an excellent singer until Numer came along.

After the merriment was over, the fellows took a little break; some went outside for a little walk, though the weather was brisk. Others simply stood around the atrium and chatted. The third part of the gathering, after sunset, was dedicated to Justin himself who was the host of the *cena*. As he had done often before, he spoke of his childhood and youth in Samaria, and how as a young man he greatly desired to discover a truth that would summarize the great teachings of the philosophers. After trying many philosophies and rejecting them, he met a certain old man one day along the seashore, though none of them could tell if he was speaking about a real man or a kind of symbol. At any rate, the man convinced Justin that only the Hebrew prophets and Jesus Christ had a truth that would completely fill his heart and his mind. Justin then told his listeners that he was also greatly impressed by the courage and heroism with which Christians faced death; he realized that they could not be evil, as they were so often portrayed. In this way he finally reached the truth he had been searching for: "When I discovered the wicked disguise which the evil spirits had thrown around the divine doctrines of the Christians to deter others from joining them, I laughed both at the authors of the falsehoods and their disguise, and at popular opinion. And I confess that I both prayed and strove with all my might to be found a Christian." [43]

He then spoke a little about the school he had begun in that very house, and the number of students and inquirers who came to his classes. Already ten of them, including a young woman, had been baptized. Like Numer, he asked the fellows to pray for some who were coming very close to the Faith, and who had asked penetrating questions in their last session. Finally he asked them all to pray for an apologetical treatise that he was writing to the Emperor Antoninus, in which he hoped to defend Christians from the charges of impiety and immorality often brought against them. "I also plan to denounce much of their own worship and their gods, which really come from the demons."

[43] From the works of St. Justin Martyr, *Apology* 2.13.

"Isn't that a little dangerous?" Titus asked. "What if they take offense and denounce you?"

"Let them do it," snapped back Justin with Middle Eastern fire in his eyes, though he was born of European parents. "Let them prove that their immoral ceremonies do not come from the devils. All the evidence is on my side."

"You're right teacher," answered Titus with an ironical smile, "but all the swords are on their side."

Nothing daunted, Justin then introduced a friend of his who had joined them for supper, and who had originally come from Jerusalem; he was an apostle [44] on his way to Britannia. "As you know," Justin began by way of introduction, "the situation has now improved on that island. Most of the fighting has stopped.[45] My friend Eleazar is going up there to spread the word of Christ, as soon as weather permits. He himself is a convert from Judaism, and was trained in the Faith by a disciple of a Christian Pharisee who knew Paul himself. There's a very small community of brethren who live on that island near the white cliffs that overlook the British shore. He surely has his work cut out for him; I know of several prophets and apostles who have already been killed by the fierce Celtic tribes living there. But he's determined to go, since Jesus said 'go forth and teach all peoples . . .'"

There was a moment of awed silence, even reverence, among Justin's students. All of them were praying for the success of Eleazar's mission. He was not an impressive-looking man, despite his obvious courage. He was rather short and balding, with a scruffy brown beard speckled with gray hairs. But the fact that he was of the same race as the Savior gave him special importance in everyone's eyes; he had received a marvelous vocation from the Messiah of his

[44] In the early Church those evangelizing distant lands were called apostles, even though they were not one of the original twelve apostles.

[45] Through the years A.D. 140–148 there had been constant battles in Britain between the native Celtic tribes and the occupying Romans.

own people. At last Philius decided to break the silence with a slightly prosaic question.

"Eleazar, do you know any Gaelic or Celtic?"

The little man, who had very bright eyes like Justin's, answered. "A Christian from Britain here in Rome has taught me a few words. I hope to get by with them for a while there, until I learn more." Then he showed them a bundle of scrolls that he was taking with him, including texts of several Hebrew prophets, a Gospel of Matthew and Mark, and four letters of Paul . . . including the one to the Galatians. He hoped to be able to translate the Gospel of Mark, the shortest one, into Celtic one day.

"Why are you taking the one to the Galatians?"

"For good fortune, because the Celts of Gaul and Britain are supposed to be related to the Galatians of Asia."

"I have one phrase in Celtic that you will surely need," said one voice in the crowd.

"What is that?"

"Listen for a moment: don't kill me yet."

It was obviously a rude, even brutal statement to make in those circumstances, but it was hard to keep from laughing. Even Eleazar himself laughed, as he shrugged off the comment. "I've prayed to the Holy Spirit," he answered, "and I trust that I can get in a few more words than that . . ."

At that point Justin invited them all to kneel and face toward the East, praying for the success of Eleazar's mission. Suddenly, without any warning, each person there heard what seemed to be a kind of strong wind rushing into the atrium, which was quite strange since the air outside was calm, and the doors and windows were shut. Eleazar, who was still standing on the platform, immediately began moving both of his arms in a circular fashion, while doing a kind of joyful dance. At first he danced in silence, but then he began to speak words, at first in a low tone of voice, but then progressively higher until he was almost shouting them. No one could understand the words. It was not Hebrew, or

Latin, or Greek . . . could it have been Celtic itself? But since there were no interpreters in the group, they could only listen and give thanks to God for what they were seeing and hearing.

After a while, when Eleazar had returned to his kneeling position and spoke no more words, Justin stood up and said that this was obviously a sign for them all to go forth, with the same Spirit that had come upon Eleazar, to bring all of Rome to Christ. He reminded them that the Eucharist the next day would be in Marius's house, and that the Pope himself would celebrate it.

That night Marcus returned to his little house with his mind whirling and his heart on fire. He had seen the gift of tongues twice before, and had met two traveling prophets, but nothing he had seen could match what he had just experienced. Numer would be staying the night at Justin's house, and Marcus was sure that the two old friends would have many things to talk about.

XXXIX.

The next day, about an hour before the sun rose, groups of families started arriving at Marius's house. A few of them were Patricians, wearing the toga or noble *palla*, others were freed men and women like Cynthia, many others were slaves. It was the moment of the Eucharist, the *agapei*, which would unite all of them in the love of the Savior, and give them the courage and energy that they needed for their daily lives.

Marcus arrived an hour earlier to help Marius and his family prepare for the service. He brought in many small cushions and stools for elderly people and women with small children to sit upon during the readings and homilies. The other people would be standing. The altar itself faced toward the East, at the part of the atrium most distant from the door. Pius arrived about a half-hour before the service, and stood at the door greeting individuals and families. He knew by name every person who entered, and gave a special blessing to those families with young children. He particularly welcomed those baptized in the previous Easter Vigil, along with the catechumens who would be staying at the Mass until the liturgy of the Eucharist.

As the service was about to begin, the men gathered at the right side of the atrium, the women at the left, putting on their veils. Cynthia had come with Carmina, who held a newborn in her arms, a little girl. Next to Cynthia was a very young woman with brown hair and a beautiful white tunic; she was wearing the garment of the neophytes. It was Portia, the equestrian girl whom Cynthia was tutoring, and who had met Scintilla in her last days.

Marcus stood with Numer, Titus, and Proclus, and a few rows in front of them stood Justin and some of his disciples. He also noticed Gaius the soldier standing to the right of him, with his son Discalus and best friend Timotheus. He knew that Gaius would sometimes go on Saturday afternoons to his father-in-law's house to pick up Timo, who would then stay overnight at Gaius's and Carmina's house, and go to Sunday Eucharist with them. Timotheus could not stand for long on his own, and after the ceremony began, he sat on one of the stools that Marcus had brought.

"May the Lord be with you," began Pope Pius, in a deep clear voice, speaking his native Latin. He was a tall rather thin man like Telesphorus, but without a beard. He invited the assembly to express sorrow for their sins, then intoned the *Kyrie Eleison*. Marcus and Numer sang it confidently with their good voices, while Titus and Proclus maintained a respectful silence. The women's voices, led by Carmina and Cynthia, were particularly beautiful . . . and Marcus concluded that the Almighty Father must be pleased by this hymn to his praise, coming from so many different kinds of people, but united in the one faith.

Afterward came the readings. A deacon that Marcus did

not know did the reading from Isaiah, followed by the responsorial psalm. It was that of the Good Shepherd (Psalm 23). After that he read a section from Paul's letter to the Romans, their home community. Finally Pius himself, accompanied by his assistant Eusebius, stood up to proclaim the Gospel. It was from the seventh chapter of Matthew, which he read in Greek: "Every one therefore who hears these words of mine and does them will be like a wise man who built his house upon the rock; and the rain fell, and the floods came, and the winds blew and beat upon that house, but it did not fall, because it had been founded on the rock. And every one who hears these words of mine and does not do them will be like a foolish man who built his house upon the sand; and the rain fell, and the floods came, and the winds blew and beat against that house, and it fell; and great was its ruin" (Mt 7: 24-27).

He then gave his sermon in Latin: "Dear brothers and sisters in Christ, the Lord's evangelist records for us a thought-provoking parable this morning. We must be like the wise man who built his house on rock. The city of Rome is built on seven hills, but our faith must be built on something much stronger: faith in Jesus Christ and his Church. If we truly believe in his saving word and sacraments, and live according to his teaching, his Holy Spirit will act within us.

"We know that the rain, the floods, and the winds will come. Perhaps even an earthquake. We can even think of the eruption of Mount Vesuvius in Pompei more than two generations ago; perhaps some of you had relatives who died there.[46] But our faith in the Lord Christ and his Way, our charity for one another will always keep the house strong. Yes, the winds will come—the winds of false prophets like Valentinus and Marcion who have deceived many; yes, the rains will come—the rains of daily disappointments and frustrations that we must all face; yes, the floods will come—floods of persecution and even death. In this regard,

---

[46] The city of Pompei was destroyed by volcanic eruption in A.D. 79.

we recall most recently how Father Atticus and some of our brothers and sisters were condemned to the mines. Perhaps even today or tomorrow some of us will be denounced and brought to trial for our faith in Christ. But we are not afraid, because our house is founded on rock, and Jesus himself said to his apostles: 'Take courage, I have overcome the world.'" [47]

"Lord, keep us strong always. Give us your grace always and send us your Spirit with the gift of fortitude. For in the end, it is not enough for us to have inspiring words and intentions, or to know the words of the Gospel. We must give the Lord our deeds and actions, in union with him. Only thus will the foundation of our lives be strong. Such is the foundation laid by Peter my predecessor and by Paul, and all of our older brothers and sisters who were killed by the Beast in that first trial.[48] Since then there have been many others . . . Linus, Cletus, Clement, Ignatius, and countless more. All are brave witnesses, all have achieved the immaculate crown of glory from Jesus, Lamb of God. Let us go often to them in our prayers, and especially to Mary the Mother of Jesus who will always intercede for us with the Father, the Son, and the Holy Spirit."

"May God bless you all, and guide you in the Way of Peace, with His Eternal Light."

Then the entire assembly answered, "Amen. Amen."

At that point the catechumens, about twenty of them, went into the courtyard, where they would receive more instruction in Christ's teachings. Father Eusebius led the prayer of the faithful, especially remembering those who had been condemned most recently, along with the sick and the needy. He made special reference to the brothers and sisters of Christ in Egypt, since he knew that Numer was present with them.

[47] John 16:33.

[48] The Emperor Nero put to death in Rome many Christian men and women in A.D. 67. See also Rev 13:18.

After that, Gaius and Carmina brought to the altar the basket of loaves and the wine that would become the Lord's body and blood. Marcus held little Discalus in his arms for Gaius, and Cynthia held the baby girl for Carmina. The great liturgy of the Eucharist was beginning.[49]

"*Te igitur, Clementissime Pater . . .*"

Cynthia particularly prayed to the eternal Father first for Pius himself and his presbyters . . . then for the catechumens she was instructing and her tutoring work with Roman families. She asked him for the grace to connect her work with the offering of his Son at the altar, for she knew that all she did had value only if it was connected with Christ's own sacrifice. At the same time Carmina was offering her daily work at home as a mother, while Gaius thought of his duty as a father and soldier of the urban cohort for the protection of the city. As the Mass continued, Marcus felt closer and closer to everyone in the room, and above all to Christ, who he knew would soon come to them in the Holy Eucharist.

"*Memento Domine, famulorum tuorum . . .*"

Marcus particularly remembered Atticus, if he were still alive, Numer, who stood right next to him, and his mother Aurelia, so that someday she too would find Jesus Christ. After his father's death they had become much closer to one another. Timotheus, standing up and leaning on Gaius, thought particularly of his parents, and his little adopted sister Tertia. He renewed his intention to offer his physical pain for their benefit, and was sorry if he had complained or become depressed at times with it.

"*Communicantes et memoriam venerantes . . .*"

Marcus's mind expanded to all in Rome. He thought particularly of Titus, Philius, and Proclus, of Justin and his

---

[49] The following Eucharistic texts in Latin are taken from the traditional Roman Canon, though it is most likely that second-century Masses in Rome were celebrated in Greek. The main substance of the ancient prayers and petitions in both languages, however, appears to be very similar.

students . . . and of all the families that he knew: Justus and Consti (who were at that moment hosting the Eucharist at their house on the road to Ostia), Gaius and Carmina, Discalus and Silvia, and so many more.

Pius then prayed for the Holy Spirit to come upon the gifts, and Marcus united himself with his petition, as he prepared himself to hear the words of the Lord at the Last Supper. They had come to the center of the Sacrifice: the Lord's body and blood were about to be made present upon the altar. "Take this all of you and eat: This is my Body, which will be given up for you," Pope Pius was pronouncing in deep clear tones. "Take this all of you and drink from it; for this is the Chalice of my Blood, of the new and everlasting covenant. . . ." The entire congregation was on its knees, looking up and adoring the sacred Body and Blood that Pius was holding up for them. Marcus renewed his dedication to God once again, this time with a special fervor because of the events of the past few days; he dedicated everything— his classes, his friendships, his own body and blood—in the service of the Lord Christ. It was a tremendous joy to have Numer, and Titus, and Philius right next to him at that moment; he was sure that each in his own way was worshipping the Lord in the Eucharist.

As the Eucharistic prayer continued, he prayed for his deceased father, entrusting him to Junia's intercession. Though he was not a Christian, he was a virtuous man, and had died with the word "God" on his lips; Marcus would never forget that. He was hearing Pius's prayer that they were all united to the great saints and martyrs who had gone before them. He particularly remembered Bishop Telesphorus and his most courageous death, and the Christian woman who had also been killed on the same day—his mother's friend Fulvia. He prayed to Fulvia for his mother.

It was the moment of the Great Amen. Marcus particularly loved to hear that part at every Mass. It was the self-giving love of Christ, which he himself was trying to imitate in his work and entire life: Through Him, with Him, in Him, in the unity of the Holy Spirit, all glory and honor is yours, Almighty Father . . ."

After they said the *Pater Noster*, Pius asked everyone to exchange the sign of peace. Marcus embraced Numer first, then Titus and Philius. Numer and Titus seemed to be closer to each other than ever, despite the closing of the Aventine House. Marcus had given the sign of peace at many Eucharists, but this time it reminded him of his first embrace of peace at the catacomb on the Via Appia, when Numer and Titus were with him. Once again the thought of Atticus flashed through his mind; he was the priest who had baptized and confirmed him, and given him his first Communion. *Atticus, Atticus, how close I am to you now . . . wherever you are!*

The moment had come for Communion. Pius and Eusebius were offering the Lord's body; a presbyter and deacon were offering his precious blood. Marcus, following Numer, stepped up to receive the Lord. They both returned to their places and knelt down on the hard but decorative floor of Marius's atrium. At that moment Marcus was oblivious to everyone around him. He could hear people walking by him, with the rustling of togas and *pallas*, with light and heavier steps, with an occasional baby's cry, but he was concentrating on only one thing: the Lord Christ Himself had come to him—his King, his Teacher, his Shepherd, his Physician, his greatest Friend.

XL.

The Eucharist was about to end. The people all stood as the successor of Peter was about to give his final blessing and dismissal. But before doing so, he made a brief announcement: "Before we go with our gifts for the poor and sick, I would invite you to remain for a short while after the final dismissal. As you know, Numer from the Church in Alexandria is visiting us for a few weeks, and is now staying with Justin at his house. I have asked him to speak to us about our brethren in Egypt, so that we can pray for all of them. He has also composed a musical piece on his flute that he would like to share with you."

Then Pius gave his final blessing, followed by the words *Ite Missa est*: "the Mass is ended; go in peace."

In the following moments the people began to speak softly to one another, as the deacons moved the table of sacrifice to the triclinium, and purified the vessels of Holy Communion. Marcus could detect an air of excitement and expectation as Numer got ready to ascend the platform. He was known in Rome by practically everyone. He had visited many families while he lived here, and had brought many young men to Christ, most of whom had married, but some of whom had chosen the path of continence for Christ's kingdom, as he had. He smiled at the assembly as he climbed the platform, his short sturdy frame exuding a kind of robust strength and confidence. He placed his flute on a small table next to him.

Then he began to speak, in simple elegant Latin with a Coptic accent, about the Church in Northeastern Africa. Many things Marcus had already heard from his personal conversations with him, and from the gathering at Justin's house the previous night. But now Numer added more information about families who were converting to the Gospel, and about the Church in the neighboring province of Cyrenaica. "In the capital city of Cyrene, there was a young woman named Celia who married the Roman governor. She was a native of Cyrenaica, from a small fishing village on the sea. She and her whole family converted to the Church when she was ten years old; a very elderly disciple of the evangelist Mark, who had known him as a boy in Alexandria, had actually given all of them instruction in the

Faith. Governor Rufinus was very taken with Celia's beauty and good sense, and married her in her eighteenth year, despite her humble birth. All the Christians of Cyrene and many in Alexandria were praying that her husband Rufinus might come to the Lord through Celia's example and prayer."

Numer had achieved the undivided attention of the assembly. It seemed to Marcus that every man and woman in the room was personally with Celia at that moment, and praying for her. The atrium was very quiet, but Numer's next sentence broke the spell.

"But it was not to be," he continued. "Just after she gave birth to their first child, a girl, her husband denounced her as a Christian. No explanation was ever given for this. He certainly knew before he married her that she was a Christian, and had placed no objection. We can only think that he became attracted to another woman, or that Celia did something to displease him. He never told her what she had done wrong. Some people of Cyrene thought that she had given him a child too quickly, or that he did not want a girl. Others say that he had been threatened politically, by one of his rivals, because his wife was a Christian."

"The whole community was praying for Celia and her little girl; there was a brief perfunctory trial, and sentence was given. She refused to offer incense to the Roman and Egyptian gods, and was sentenced to be devoured by lions in the amphitheatre just outside of the capital." Numer's voice began to weaken and break: he forced himself to say "to the end her courage . . ." but he couldn't go on, and began to weep. It was an awkward moment, but then, without any prompting, one of the women in the assembly began singing a little hymn to the Lord Christ, while others joined her. Marcus knew that it was the Holy Spirit working. He had heard a similar melody sung at assemblies before, but this time the woman included the name "Celia" and her victory for Christ. At the end of the hymn, when he had recovered from his emotion, Numer stated that Celia had the joy of seeing her little girl baptized with the name Perpetua, and confirmed in the Holy Spirit. She was then given to a Christian family in Alexandria, with whom she would live and be raised. Celia's final prayer was for the soul of her husband, and for the perseverance of her little girl in the Faith.

The assembly was silent for a few moments after Numer spoke. In a way, what he had said was not new to any of them. Being Christians, they had all known people in very similar circumstances; many of them had already lost loved ones, both men and women, young and old, who had been sent to the Colosseum or condemned to the mines. But there was something particularly poignant in Celia's story, because she had been born and raised in a poor family, and had achieved such a high social position—while remaining true to Christ until the end.

After he had spoken, some of the women, including Cynthia and Carmina, intoned another hymn of praise to the Lord Christ. It asked Celia to pray for them, and included a petition for all Christians in Northeast Africa. Marcus had never heard the hymn before, but he knew that the Spirit was making it happen, just as he had done with the previous canticle.

When the hymn was finished, Numer, still standing on the platform, deftly took up the flute on the table. He looked relaxed but intent at the same time. As he began to play his instrument, the music seemed to flow from his mind and his heart in a very natural way. It was obviously something that he had worked upon for a long time; it had no exaggerated notes or flourishes, but did have a recurring melody that was very pleasant, which reminded Marcus of a Chaldaean shepherd's song that he had once heard. Blended into that central melody was a series of quick and lively notes, mixed with slower sadder ones. The listener had the overall impression of something light and charming penetrated by something deep and sorrowful. The combined effect was very beautiful, and Marcus in some way thought that the tune was much like life itself, with its same day-to-day melody, but mysteriously mixed with joys and sorrows.

Everyone in the atrium, including the children, were drawn into the music. Some of them looked serious as they heard it, some of them smiled, and a few others wept. But at one point, when it seemed that the tune might be reaching a crescendo, Numer stopped playing the flute, and began to speak.

"Dear brothers and sisters, I have been working on this melody for many years, ever since I became a Christian. I have not given it a name; perhaps I never can. But every note of it reminds me of Jesus Christ, my love and my all. He is with me every day of my life, in ordinary things, in happy things, and in sad things—and he alone knows the ending of the song. I can only wish that each of you will also find him in your daily life, for he is truly the Way, the Truth, and the Life. Please pray for me."

XLI.

Numer stayed in the city for the next two months. He visited a few families, but remained mostly with his old friends from the Aventine House. Several times he met with fellows at Marcus's house; somehow they all fit into that little area that he called home. The African spoke often of his dream for his native city of Alexandria. He dreamed of a great Academy of learning that could begin there, which would incorporate the best of Greek insights, particularly Plato's, with the best of Christian teaching. Since Alexandria was the intellectual capital of the world, this school would draw students from around the Empire, and be a great influence in the service of Christ.

"But who will be the philosophy teachers? Most philosophers now laugh at Christianity," Philius asked incredulously.

"I don't know," Numer said confidently, "but someday they'll come. And when they come, people won't laugh at us anymore."

Marcus brought Numer many times to see his mother, who was now living alone in the big estate on the Esquiline. She had thought briefly of remarrying, but she wanted to remain in mourning for a year after Gaius's death, following the pious custom of widows in times of the Old Republic. She had actually invited Marcus to have some of his gatherings at her house, bringing Numer and others, but he did not want to expose her to the charge of harboring Christians. Aurelia was always delighted when Numer came to visit: she loved his jokes and songs on the flute. She was impressed by his cosmopolitan ways, and particularly marveled that he—being from the most sophisticated city in the world and center of Greek culture—was still a rather simple and straightforward person. On one visit she had even been on the verge of asking him about how he became a Christian, but she was afraid and held back.

A few weeks later, in the month of February, Marcus invited his African friend to the baths with Titus. As they did before, they avoided the tepidarium, and went directly to the gymnasium to play *trigon*, which was a very sophisticated game of catch. Titus came in first, mostly because of his superior height, followed by Numer and Marcus. Being a bit miffed at finishing third, Marcus invited them to a wrestling match, but he had no takers. Even Numer had given up trying to beat him. "But I will take you up on a brisk dip in the frigidarium," Numer offered, so they all jumped into the frigid water after they had removed the perspiration from their bodies.

Titus went to his family's home after the Baths, while Marcus and Numer walked together along the streets of the city. They passed the Pantheon, that huge monument to the pagan gods built by Hadrian twelve years before, and said a prayer for the conversion of those entering it. Aferward they had some wine at Marcus's favorite tavern near the Via Biberatica. "In a month or so," Numer said, "when the weather is a little better, I should try to make my way to Brindisium. One of my students is from there, and wants to introduce me to his family. He is seriously considering Christ and his teaching. From there I should make my way to Corinth, across the Adriatic, to visit another student and his family. He has written to me recently that he wants to become a catechumen."

"Do you have to leave so soon?" Marcus asked, obviously disappointed.

"I think my work is done here for now," his friend answered, "and the Lord is calling me to another vineyard. When it's safe to travel, I'll return to Egypt."

Marcus said nothing, still having a bit of his Stoic father in him, and tried to mask his sorrow at the news. He knew that many others, including his mother, would also be disappointed. But he knew that Numer would have to leave at some point; it was God's will for him.

They went on to speak about the students that Marcus was teaching at the Athenaeum, and Numer shared some ideas on how to get them thinking about Christianity, or drop their prejudices against it. Marcus thought it was a good moment to speak about Servianus, who was not his student, but his friend and colleague. He told him that he was very drawn to the ideas of Valentinus and Marcion, and that he hadn't been able to convince him that Christ was truly divine and had become a man of real flesh and blood.

Numer rested his head in his hands for a minute, and moved his lips slowly, as if he were praying. "I have a feeling," he said presently, "that he will be baptized in the end, and will come to the true Church. But he has to see and experience the greatness of Christ incarnate . . . in the flesh . . . in order to overcome this silly 'gnosis' that has captivated him. Why not invite him to visit one of the poor families in the Subura district, as you and I did after the last Eucharist?"

"Agreed," Marcus said. He had never thought of that approach. "And as far as my students, where do you think would be a good place for me to meet with them, and speak about the Christ? We don't have the Aventine house anymore, and I don't want to use my mother's home. I was thinking of just crowding them into my house."

"Good. The walls of the Athenaeum have eyes and ears. Can you bring three fellows to the Master by October?"

"I'll try," his friend answered. Marcus felt badly that he hadn't tried very hard to bring his students to Christianity in the past, with the excuse of being "cautious." He had established himself as an excellent teacher of Platonism, but had spoken very little about the Christ to anyone except Servianus.

"What has always helped me," Numer added, "is to remember what the Apostle said: *caritas Christi urget nos*.[50] It's God's love that is strongest, in the end; it conquers all obstacles. And speaking of love, do you still have that hair shirt that you wore before coming into the Church?"

"Yes, but I rarely use it," Marcus answered with sincerity.

"Well, why don't you wear it more, and offer it for your students? It will connect you more with Christ and his cross . . ."

Marcus laughed a bit and said that he would.

Within four weeks Numer left for Brindisium. He gave Marcus a quick strong embrace, just before the *raeda* was leaving. No long or tearful goodbyes; that was not Numer's style. But as Marcus watched the carriage heading East on the road to Brindisium across the peninsula, he had the sudden premonition that he would never see his best friend again, at least in this world.

---

[50] 2 Cor 5:14.

THE JOY OF A NEW LIFE

XLII.

Séptimus and Gaius were becoming good friends, apart from being brothers in Christ. Since both of them shared the same military training ground, they would often chat after their drills and exercises, or go with their friends to a local tavern. At times fights would break out there between the soldiers, often the effect of too much wine. A few times some of the men went to visit a brothel after drinks, but Gaius and Séptimus would never go with them, and tried to dissuade them. They would often be ridiculed for that, but not too much, because both Gaius and Séptimus were excellent fighters, and the men knew that. Twice Gaius had actually convinced a couple of the men to go home to their wives and children right away. He would often talk in glowing terms about his own three children, and Séptimus would speak about his four children.

As they were walking home one afternoon (they both lived in the same area of Rome, near the Janiculum), Séptimus brought up some surprising news for Gaius. "My commander Quintus would like to meet you and your family. He is of course very grateful for what you did for him on the day of Caesar's entry into the city."

"I was only doing my duty."

"Yes, and you have a big wound on your left shoulder to prove it," answered his older friend.

"Oh, that," Gaius casually waved his hand. "It's quite healed by now. I should be grateful; my best friend Timotheus's wounds have never healed."

"All the same," Séptimus continued, "I think you should

accept Quintus's request. I've been praying for him for a long time, and we have become good friends. He knows that my family and I are Christians, but he doesn't care. He has actually been asking me more questions about Christ and his teaching recently. As you know he has never lost his fascination and admiration for Junia, and how bravely she died."

"I also remain fascinated," replied Gaius, "though I was only a little lad on my father's shoulders when I saw her being carried to her death. But to answer your question: yes, I would be happy and honored to receive Quintus as a guest, and I'm sure that Carmina will feel the same."

Within a week Quintus, Prefect of the Praetorian Guard, was knocking at the door of Gaius's little house near the Janiculum. He was not in military uniform, but was wearing a simple gray tunic and a clean perfectly pleated toga. Carmina had seen Quintus in military processions in the city but had never met him personally. He was a tall man with curly dark hair and in perfect physical shape. Carmina and Gaius's stepmother Silvia had totally cleaned and dusted the small house, and had prepared a simple but tasty meal of chicken, cooked vegetables, and freshly baked bread with a special sauce that Silvia learned to make from her mother.

Quintus had not visited a plebeian home in many years, and was a little taken aback when Gaius himself opened the door, with five-year-old Discalus standing at his side. In his elaborate home on the Esquiline, slaves always opened the door. Gaius raised his arm to salute him, but Quintus deftly intercepted his arm and gave him a strong Roman arm shake, right forearm to right forearm. He was smiling broadly, and seemed genuinely delighted to be paying him a visit.

Gaius introduced him to Carmina, who gave him a gracious smile. She was dressed in a light blue tunic, and had a small yellow flower in her smooth brown hair. She was holding her son Justus, just two months old, in her left arm.

Little Drusilla stood shyly behind her, peering up at the stranger. Gaius's stepmother Silvia, dressed in a simple white tunic, bowed slightly to him after she was introduced. She wore a light green apron since she was just putting some dressing on the chicken.

Quintus bowed to both of the ladies, which quite surprised them, since he was an Equestrian and they were only plebeians. "Please forgive me if I ask you a very direct question at first," he said to Carmina, "but how do you manage to keep track of these three children, and still look so young and happy?"

Carmina blushed a bit as she moved a step closer to Gaius.

"I don't know if you would understand, sir," she said shyly, as she looked into his clear gray eyes.

"Please try me," Quintus said.

"First I go each day to the children's angels."

"Angels. Yes, I've heard of them. Is that a Christian belief?"

"Yes," Carmina answered, "they're really the protecting spirits of our home and children. Whenever I feel a bit nervous or impatient about something, I go to them, and they always make me feel calm and find an answer for me."

"It's true, sir," Gaius added playfully. "And one of her angels is right behind her now, my stepmother Silvia. She helps Carmina a lot with the children, so that she can get her beauty sleep."

At that Carmina and Silvia laughed, after which Carmina gave Gaius a little shove on his arm, pretending that she was indignant.

As Gaius and Quintus were about to recline at the triclinium couch, and Carmina and the children were sitting at a wooden table near the stove—Gaius told his superior that he was going to say some prayers and bless the meal, before they ate. Séptimus had told him that Quintus would not be surprised if he did this. So Gaius led the prayer as he always did, giving thanks for the food and praying to the Lord Christ for their guest in a special way.

Quintus felt truly relaxed with this family. He could be himself, and did not have to put on airs, or try to defend himself—as he often had to do when he dined with other Equestrians or Patricians. As the meal progressed, with a few timely questions from Gaius and Carmina, he found himself speaking freely about his work, the Emperor's plans, and his home. He also had many questions for them, not only about Gaius and the urban cohort, but about Carmina's parents and her family.

"I heard from Séptimus that your parents adopted a little girl. Is she doing well?"

"Oh, yes," Carmina answered, "she's a year older than Discalus, and has a mind of her own. My mother Constantia is teaching her to read now."

"I also know that you have a brother named Timotheus, who was stabbed many years ago in a school here. They should have arrested and punished his attackers, but being a Christian family, I suppose there was nothing more that you could do. You and your parents must have suffered greatly, Carmina."

"Yes, we did, but Timotheus never complained about it. His attitude has helped us tremendously as a family over the years. I feel privileged to be his sister."

"How did you know about Timotheus, sir?" Gaius asked.

"You must know that as head of the Praetorian Guard I have to know everything about everyone. Yes, and Séptimus is my 'Christian spy.' He tells me everything, and I tell him everything!" They all laughed at that, and felt even more at ease with him as the evening unfolded.

But Quintus could not seem to take his eyes off the children. He was particularly impressed with little Discalus, a stout strong boy of five, who was riding on a wooden horse that Gaius had made for him. He was pretending that he was going into battle, and kept shouting commands at his little sister Drusilla, who was sitting right next to him and completely ignoring him, as she played with a little woolen doll with blonde hair that her grandmother Consti had made for her.

"What's the boy's name?" Quintus asked.

"Discalus, after his grandfather."

"I can see from his bearing on the wooden horse that he has the makings of a good soldier, a credit to your family name of Quinctius."

Carmina looked down to the floor, with a slightly troubled look on her face. It was a sore point between her and Gaius, for he wanted their son to be a soldier, but she wanted him to go into business someday like her father Justus.

Quintus did not notice their uneasiness, but walked over to the boy, and suddenly lifted him from the toy horse into his strong arms. The boy at first screamed and protested, but then he saw the friendly smile on Quintus's face, and his father's reassuring look—so he quickly relaxed in his arms. Quintus lifted him high above his head and shook him; then he put the boy down slowly back onto his horse, giving him a kiss on his forehead. As he returned to the dining couch, Gaius and Carmina could see tears in his eyes, though he was trying to wipe them away. Carmina was shocked when she saw it, but Gaius was not, remembering one of his conversations with Séptimus.

Quintus quickly recovered and began to speak more about his home on the Esquiline, and his wife Claudia. Then, completely unexpectedly, he said to Gaius, "I would like to invite you and Carmina to *cena* (supper) in my home in two weeks. I would very much like you to meet my wife, Claudia."

Gaius wanted to say yes immediately, but he noticed a look of hesitation on his wife's face. She had heard that Claudia was quite anti-Christian and had been a close friend of Livia, who had conspired with her mother to condemn Marcus's sister.

"One moment, sir. I would like to speak with my wife about it."

At first Quintus was surprised at Gaius's answer. Wasn't Gaius in charge of the house; why did he have to ask his wife about it? But then he said, "Yes, I understand; I am sorry that I asked you so abruptly."

After speaking with Carmina in the other room for a few minutes, Gaius returned to his guest looking more at ease. "Yes sir, we would be honored to visit you and lady Claudia in your home. I suppose that you would only want me and my wife for this occasion."

"Oh, no," the Prefect answered quickly and vehemently, as if giving a military command, "please bring your children also . . . *all* of them!"

XLIII.

The next day Carmina went to see Cynthia at her small house near the Viminal Hill. Though Carmina had heard about Junia's former slave from her Christian friends, she met her for the first time only a year before at the school for orphan girls named the Faustinianae, in honor of the Emperor's deceased wife. Carmina had volunteered to take care of the girls for an afternoon a week, and to sing for them. She had met Cynthia there, who was teaching them to read. It was a marvelous coincidence, since Cynthia had heard from Junia, years before, of the Christian family who had a little girl that had witnessed her baptism in the catacomb. But she had never met Carmina. "So you're the one," Cynthia joked, "you're the one who picked up those apples on the street with Junia when you were eight years old!" Since then, they had visited with each other frequently. Carmina considered the freed woman to be like an older sister for her. She had such good advice about prayer and teaching children, and would often encourage her if she felt a little down or nervous about things. Carmina knew that she was one of the *virgines* who had given up everything for Christ.

"I'm so excited," Carmina began telling her, "Quintus, Prefect of the Praetorian Guard, has asked Gaius and me—and all the children—to visit him and his wife Claudia at their estate on the Esquiline, on the calends of next month."

Cynthia's dark eyes lit up when she heard the news, as if she had just discovered an opportunity that she had been seeking for a long time. Carmina then went on to narrate how Gaius had met Quintus, how he had saved him from assassins, and how Quintus had visited them for *cena*. She told Cynthia that she had been particularly amazed to see tears in his eyes after he picked up little Discalus.

"I think I know the reason for that," Cynthia said.

"What is it?"

"If I tell you, will you simply keep it in your prayer, and not tell anyone else?"

"I will."

"Quintus always wanted to have a son. But early in their marriage their first child was stillborn. It was very hard on Claudia, and she has never wanted to have another child. For years I've tried to encourage her again and again to trust in God and his goodness, and to give her husband a child, but she has not been willing."

"So that's why Quintus had tears in his eyes; he wants to have a son, but cannot have one."

"Yes, and knowing Quintus, he's too noble to divorce Claudia and take another wife. I don't think that he has even taken a mistress."

Carmina looked down at the simple mosaic on the floor in Cynthia's entranceway: a ship with white sails moving toward the sun. She said a silent prayer for Quintus and Claudia.

"What do you think, Cynthia? Is there anything that Gaius and I can do to help the situation? The supper is in two weeks. I'm sure that if I said anything or tried to convince her, it would seem strange to her, or only make things worse."

"I have an idea," the Greek woman said, as she rubbed her forehead with her right hand. Then she invited Carmina to sit down, and they spoke for a about an hour.

After that the two women embraced, and Cynthia said, "The peace of Christ be with you, Carmina. I ask you to pray especially in the next two weeks to Mary Mother of Jesus, for what we just spoke about. I'm sure that it will need prayer in order to work. And I'll be especially asking your angel to help you on the day of your *cena* with them."

XLIV.

The home of Quintus and Claudia on the Esquiline was one of the best appointed and efficient estates in Rome. Claudia had always been an excellent manager, and knew how to get things done. She also had very good taste in decorations: her mosaics and frescos were admired by many of the wealthiest families in Rome. The slaves were punctual in their duties, and Claudia worked well with them—though at times she would give in to bad temper and have one of them whipped.

She was around thirty years of age now, a tall, attractive woman with a kind of queenly presence about her. Being the wife of the Prefect of the Praetorian Guard, one of the most important positions in the city, she hosted many dinners and parties, where she had always managed to capture the center of people's attention by her wit and shrewd commentaries. Unlike other wealthy women, however, she would not permit drunkenness or sexual promiscuity in her home—partly because of Cynthia's influence, partly because of Quintus's own desires in the matter.

But there was something that seemed remote and sad about her; she had few really close friends, except for Livia and Cynthia. Recently she and Quintus had also quarreled about things, and she was feeling more distant from him.

When she heard of Quintus's invitation of Gaius and his family to their home, she was annoyed. "They are not Patricians or Equestrians. Both are children of merchants," she complained. "Yes, it's true," Quintus answered. "But nobility is best measured by words and actions, not by family blood lines. You know the great favor that Gaius did for me on the day of the Emperor's parade. He is actually part of the noble line of Quinctius, related by adoption to Cincinnatus, though his family fell on harder times over the years."

Claudia could answer nothing to that; of course she was very grateful for Gaius's saving of her husband, and had always desired to meet him. Since she suspected that the family was Christian however, she decided to maintain a certain reserve in dealing with them, while fulfilling her duty as a hostess. She did not want her husband to get involved with them. Already he was known as a Christian sympathizer, since he had refused to act on two denunciations against Séptimus, his head charioteer.

The day arrived for the supper. Gaius had gotten the afternoon off from cohort duty, and his family arrived at Quintus's door about the tenth hour of the day, a couple of hours before sunset. Quintus sent a special carriage and driver for the family, who took them from their house to his estate on the Esquiline, which was actually not far from the house of deceased Senator Gaius. As they passed the beautiful white marble mansion, Carmina said a prayer to Junia for her mother Aurelia and brother Marcus. After Junia's death she had prayed to her for many things: she knew that Junia had great power with God, as a virgin and martyr. Carmina always felt a fascination for her, ever since she had met her that day in the catacombs.

For the occasion Claudia wore a light purple *palla* with a gold brooch on her left shoulder. She decided not to have an elaborate hairdo, but simply had her front locks curled a bit, with a small silver garland on her head. Carmina had purchased a new tunic for the occasion with a light blue cape;

like all Christian women, she wore no jewelry. Her hair was smooth and beautifully combed, with a small yellow ribbon that went well with her light brown eyes.

As they entered Quintus's home, little Discalus was very impressed with the atrium, especially the bright red and yellow mosaics on the wall. He excitedly asked his parents what each picture was; he particularly liked one with an athlete running around a bull. The fountain in the *peristylium* (courtyard) was an object of instant interest for both children: Discalus wanted to jump in, while Drusilla simply went up to the water to look at her reflection, and dip her hand into it. Little Justus, three months old, slept peacefully in his mother's arms, as he would do for most of the evening.

After viewing the fountain, Quintus invited the family into his study, at the center of which stood a large green marble table, with various scrolls neatly tied and placed to one side. At the center of the table was a large page with the names of different Praetorian guards, and where they were stationed at the moment. Quintus explained to his guests that he had to update this list each day, according to their various assignments and the Emperor's orders. On the wall in front of the table was a large detailed map of Rome, with all of its streets, temples, and market places. It was the largest map of the city that Gaius had ever seen. On one side of his study was a bust of the Emperor Antoninus, and on the other side, the bust of a square-faced man with pursed lips and an intense look in his eyes. "This is the bust of my father, Cassianus," Quintus told his guests proudly. "He was highly honored by Hadrian, and one of his best generals. Behind his bust on the wall are some of the weapons that he used during the war in Dacia, for which he became famous." As Gaius looked, he could see the *gladius*, the two-edged sword used by all Roman legionaries; the *scutum*, the four-foot-long shield embossed with bronze; the *pilum*, a six-foot-long javelin with a wooden shaft and iron point; the *galea*, the steel helmet decorated with gold pieces and a red plume; and the *lorica*, Cassianus's armor, which included a steel breastplate with straps of bronze and leather. On a little stand to the right of the weapons was a long staff with a bright red flag bearing the image of an eagle in the center: it was the standard used by Cassianus's legion.

Gaius and Discalus could not take their eyes off so many military treasures. Gaius asked Quintus a few questions about his father and some of the battles he had waged, which Quintus answered succinctly. He could have spent the entire evening speaking of these battles, but he knew his guests must be hungry. Little Discalus wanted to pull down the *gladius* and handle it, but he could not reach it. Quintus only laughed: "Some day, young man, when you're a little older. But we must not let your mother worry." Carmina, with Claudia standing next to her, had watched the whole scene with mixed feelings. She realized, as every Roman did, that it was her army that had made Rome great, and extended her power throughout the known world. In one way she was proud of her city's accomplishment, but personally she had reservations about the many wars waged by Rome. Didn't the Lord say to "turn the other cheek, and do good to those who hate you"? So she simply smiled, and asked a few polite questions of her host.

As Claudia got to know her guests, she felt more and more at ease with them. There were no mocking comments, no obscene innuendos, no desire to show any kind of superiority—as she was used to seeing in her other guests. She had heard of Gaius's excellent reputation as a fighter in the cohort, but he said nothing of his accomplishments, and simply listened to Quintus. What really surprised her was that he, the man of the family, helped Carmina take care of the children: he even took little Justus in his arms when he was fussing a bit in the study. Carmina said little, but Claudia could note by the content of her questions and the look in her eyes that she was a very intelligent person, with a great sensitivity. She particularly noticed how kind and attentive she was to herself, as if she already knew her in some way.

When they arrived to the triclinium, the slaves had already prepared the first course. There were figs and olives from Cyprus, and a fine wine from Southern Gaul. At the center of the table was a delicacy that Gaius and Carmina had never seen: minced lobster balls and oysters served in a very tasty sauce, with bits of fresh bread surrounding them. Their hosts went to the table and began to eat right away, but Gaius and Carmina looked at each other in a perplexed kind of way, as if not knowing what to do. Their children were not eating either.

"What's wrong?" Claudia asked. "Are the figs and wine not acceptable?"

"Oh, yes, of course they are," Gaius answered, feeling very embarrassed. "But our family has the custom of saying a little prayer before we eat."

"Really?" Claudia asked ironically. Then she added a little maliciously since she suspected that they were Christians: "A prayer to the gods of Rome, perhaps?"

"Oh, no," five-year-old Discalus then blurted out in a loud, almost triumphant voice. "The gods of Rome are a big fake. We say a prayer to the real God and his Son Jesus Christ—to bless our meal and our family." Then he turned and asked Gaius: "Father, can I say the prayer today?"

There was a moment of awkward silence. Gaius and Carmina did not know what to say, and looked at each other with desperation. Quintus sat perfectly still for a moment, not knowing what to do. Then suddenly, most unexpectedly Claudia began to laugh, clapping her hands as if she had heard a funny joke. "Oh, yes, little Discalus," she said, "please lead us all in your Christian prayer."

So the little boy began: "Lord God of Heaven and earth, please bless the food that we're about to eat, but especially bless General Quintus and his very nice wife Claudia, through Jesus Christ our Lord. Amen."

At that point all the adults laughed and praised the little boy. Quintus picked him up and kissed him, and Claudia patted him on the top of his head. The rest of the meal was delightful for everyone. Quintus had never seen his wife in a better mood, not since their honeymoon. She began to speak to Carmina about her personal life: that she was an only child, that she had always wanted to have a brother or sister, but that her parents never gave her one. She even alluded to the child that she had lost, and the sorrow that this had caused her. She asked Carmina all kinds of questions about her parents and her brother, about each child that she had, and how she took care of them all. As a matter of fact, she and Carmina were talking so much that Quintus and Gaius simply looked at each other and shrugged their shoulders.

At the end of the meal, which featured different kinds of fruit and honey, a Syrian flautist whom Claudia had hired walked into the room, sat on a stool near the table, and began to play a slow dancing tune from Antioch. Discalus and Drusilla immediately got up from the table and went to the middle of the room, where they began to dance with each other, as little children do. Everyone laughed, and clapped their hands in time with the music. Then the adults got up and joined them: Quintus and Claudia, Gaius and Carmina. It was the first time that Quintus had danced with his wife in a long time.

When the dance was over and the flautist had left, Carmina opened a leather bag that she had set next to Justus, who was sleeping on a little woolen mat that she had brought. She pulled a small lyre from the bag, and began to tune it.

"We're so grateful to you, Quintus and Claudia, for the wonderful *cena* that you have given us. Now I would like to play for you a little song that I have composed about families. It's based on a country song from Old Republic times that my father used to sing to me when I was small; he heard it from his father in a little farming town in Latium."

"*Bene! Bene! Procede! Procede!*" (Good! Go Ahead!), all the adults cheered together, as they sat back on their couches to listen. Discalus and Drusilla went back to their little wooden table next to them, where they too prepared to listen to their mother's song, while nibbling at small pieces of bread and honey.

The song had many archaic Latin words, but was still understandable for all the adults. It spoke of fields and sheep, wheat and grapes, and, above all, the love between husband, wife, and children. In one refrain the wife praises her husband as "the protector of the family, who brings in the grain, leading us through the darkest storms," and the husband in turn praises his wife as the "joy and heart of his home, the beautiful vine that gives forth such good fruit." Interspersed throughout the song was a humorous country refrain, in the form of an old kitchen recipe:

> *Just take a little garlic,*
> *and put it in the brew*
> *from tears and love and laughter*
> *you'll make a family stew.*

Everyone was singing the catchy little refrain, including the children; they loved it. After Carmina's tune, Quintus and Gaius—not to be outdone by her—stood up and sang a marching song used extensively in the Roman army, for which everyone applauded. They applauded even more as both men kept singing and began to walk in perfect cadence around the room, in the military way. Following that, there were more songs and jokes, and more laughter.

The night had begun. It was well after sunset, and Gaius knew it was time to take the children home. He could see that his hosts really didn't want them to leave, but the hour was getting late for the little ones, so Quintus gave orders for the *raeda* to be brought to the front.

It was at that point that Discalus said: "Can I give Aunt Claudia my gift now?'

"*Aunt* Claudia?" the mistress of the house exclaimed, almost squealing with delight at the little fellow.

His mother answered: "Yes, Discalus, now's the time."

The small boy then took from his mother's leather bag a little wooden soldier that his uncle Timotheus had whittled for him. It was the statue of a Roman legionary about six inches tall, painted in full color, with a bright red plume on his helmet. "Uncle Timo whittled it, but I painted it," Discalus said proudly as he walked up to the mistress of the house. Claudia was seated on a chair near one of the couches, and as the small boy approached her, she found herself looking at him intensely, almost longingly. "This is for you," he said as he handed her the little soldier. "Oh, thank you," she said with a warm smile. But Discalus was not finished. "Can I give you a hug?" he asked, as he looked up at her. Without a word Claudia took him into her lap, and Discalus turned and hugged her, kissing her twice on her face. "Is it my turn now, Mommy?" Drusilla asked. "Yes," her mother said. Then the little girl walked up to her and bowed, presenting her with a bouquet of roses that her mother had cut for her from a papyrus scroll, with white, red, and gold colors. As Claudia bent down to take them, the little girl hugged her and kissed her, too.

After the children had gone back to Carmina, Quintus's wife was speechless. She sat perfectly still, then tried to say something, but could not. Tears began to roll down her face, and she started to sob uncontrollably. "Oh, thank you, thank you," she kept repeating as her voice began to fade. "I'm so sorry . . . please forgive me. Oh, thank you, thank you," she said once again, but her voice was too hoarse to continue, and she began to cry even more. Gaius expressed concern to Quintus about his wife, but he gently motioned that it was better for the family to go now, and they quietly left the room.

"Why is she crying, Mother?" the children asked Carmina, as they were walking to the front door, where the *raeda* was waiting for them. "Only she and God know that," Carmina answered.

And while they were traveling back to their small home near the Janiculum, the whole family said a prayer to Jesus and his Mother for both Quintus and Claudia, and for their happiness together.

About a month later Séptimus reported to Quintus's office just after sunrise, as he always did, to receive the orders of the day. The Prefect was bent over a scroll, writing down some dates and numbers, but looked up immediately as Séptimus entered the room. When Séptimus saluted him, Quintus simply looked backed at him, with a broad grin on his face. He had never seen his commander so happy. It seemed to Séptimus that he had lost fifteen years to his age, and there was a twinkle in his eye.

"Rejoice with me, Séptimus," his commander said. "My wife is expecting a child."

LOVE AND RISK

XLV.

After Numer left for Brindisium, Marcus felt newly motivated to be Christ's apostle, especially with Servianus and his students and colleagues at the Athenaeum. He began to pray more for them, in addition to fasting on Wednesdays and Fridays as all Roman Christians did. He also began to wear a hair shirt under his tunic for a time each day, in order to gain grace for them. He first thought of Servianus, his boyhood friend; he had to do something to renew their friendship. Though Servianus had been avoiding him, Marcus went up to him the next day after classes and said: "No more religious discussions for now, dear friend. Let's simply do some good for a person who needs it. I know of an old man, who just lost his wife of fifty years, and who feels quite alone and desolate." Given those terms, Servianus, who had a generous heart despite his confused ideas, could not refuse Marcus's invitation. They agreed on a day and went to a small brown house not far from the new forum.

After knocking on the wooden door, they heard a slow shuffling of feet on the other side, and Appius finally appeared—a man of nearly seventy years of age, heavily wrinkled in his face, and totally bald except for a tiny wisp of hair on the top. He looked tired and depressed, but his eyes lit up when he saw Marcus, and what he was bringing to him: figs from Dalmatia, and wine from Umbria. From previous visits Marcus knew that he enjoyed them. He invited both his visitors into the one room that served as his kitchen, dining room, and atrium . . . where Marcus and Servianus sat on two wooden stools near the table.

Marcus introduced his friend and invited Appius to speak about his life, though he had heard about it before. He had been a wine merchant in the city for many years. He and his wife Cassia had tried to have children of their own, but could not. They finally adopted a child, a boy from an unwed mother in the Subura district, but he had been born very weak and died of an illness when he was only four years old. "He had never been very healthy," Appius explained, "probably because of his mother's life and behavior." Both he and Cassia had heard about Christianity at the beginning of Trajan's reign from a merchant friend of his, a Jewish Christian from Ephesus, and they were both baptized shortly after Ignatius's death at the Colosseum. As Christians, they decided to devote their time and money to helping the poor in Rome, rather than adopting another child. As the years went by, they had become so close that his wife's sudden death five months before had been a tremendous blow to him. He had become depressed and sold his large fine house on the Janiculum; he decided to live alone, after giving most of his funds to Pope Pius for the Church.

After both young men commended him for his generosity, Marcus, hoping to keep the conversation going, asked him about his younger days.

"You must have been a young man during Domitian's time, Appius; how were things then?"

"Yes, Domitian was a fierce enemy of the Christians, and many were put to death under him. But I didn't care much for anything besides myself then. I didn't know God, and I hadn't met Cassia. I only knew the gods and goddesses of Rome."

"Did you play or enjoy any sport?" Servianus asked.

"My greatest sport was making money . . . but I did learn how to wrestle."

"Really?" Marcus exclaimed, "So did my father."

"Frankly," Appius continued with a regretful little laugh,

"I haven't been able to get out much; someday I would love to see a wrestling match again."

"Well," Marcus answered with uplifted eyebrows, as he looked significantly at Servianus, "perhaps that could be arranged. Do you have a woolen cover or mat to put on the floor?"

"Yes," the old man said with a certain enthusiasm in his voice, "I can put two of my woolen blankets together for you."

As he went to go for the blankets, Servianus made a grimace. "We haven't wrestled since we were boys, Marcus. I don't remember how."

"That's all right, Servianus, it's all part of the show. I won't hurt you, don't worry. I think it will make the old man laugh a bit."

After they spread the blankets to the floor, he and Marcus locked arms and bodies, and Servianus found himself thrown down to the blankets in three different ways. His arm was wrenched backward, his head was twisted down, and once he had the wind knocked out of him.

Appius clapped and whistled during the performance, and at the end he commented: "Marcus, you're quite good; you remind me a bit of the great Vitonius during Domitian's time. But really it's not a fair match; your friend's lighter than you, and obviously not in training."

Servianus, with wounded limbs and wounded pride, was about to agree with the old man, but in good sportsmanship he smiled and said that even as boys Marcus was able to beat him.

"But Servi always beats me in horse racing," Marcus added, in order to soothe his friend's feelings a bit.

The man thanked Marcus and Servianus profusely for having come. He was smiling and joking with them as he took them to the door. "When's your next visit?" he asked them expectantly, though they could not give him a specific day.

XLVI.

During the next week Marcus felt badly about the embarrassment he had caused Servianus. Though he was a good sport, his friend had left the old man's house in obvious pain. Yet to his surprise, after their little visit to the old man, Servi seemed more open and friendly to him than before. Their unusual adventure seemed to have changed something between them; though he did not know the reason, Marcus gave thanks. He prayed for his friend more intensely, and even began to consider his next conversation with him about the Lord Christ. But he didn't know how to bring it up, since it had long been a point of contention between them.

About two weeks afterward, something happened that astonished the son of Gaius. For the first time in several years Servianus actually came up to him after a lecture, and invited him to a horseback ride in the hills beyond the Via Flaminia. The next day after classes they were mounted on their mares, Marcus on a white spotted one, and Servianus on a light brown one. As before, they raced along the hills, and, as usual, Servianus rode faster because he was lighter, and slightly more skillful than Marcus.

"Now we're even," Servianus said with a little smile, after he had won the race by half a length.

Marcus nodded his head. "*Bene dixisti*," [51] he said, "though I still think we should put a twenty-pound bag on your horse so that our weights are the same."

Servianus laughed and pointed to a fallen log near the edge of the woods where they could sit and talk for a while. It was very close to the place where nearly ten years earlier he had warned Marcus about his father's plot against him. As they dismounted, it was almost dusk. The shadows of the trees gently enfolded them, while the sun played a game of hide and seek between the rustling leaves.

[51] Latin for "you have said the truth."

"Marcus," Servianus began, "I have something rather important to tell you."

"Go ahead," said his friend, not knowing what to expect.

"Two things have affected me greatly in the last three weeks. One was our visit to Appius. I do think that we brought back some joy into his life, Marcus, and we didn't do it by giving him a philosophical theory about the one and the many. We did it by some figs and wine, and a rather painful wrestling match—especially for me. It was all very *material*, so to speak."

Marcus laughed, and apologized once again for his rough moves.

"That's all right, Marcus. The whole thing taught me a lesson. For the first time I could see the power of the real Christ at work, something that I've been struggling with for years in my mind: namely, how the Christ could be true God and true man at the same time. I have seen now that he is not some kind of idea or mystical apparition, as Valentinus teaches, but a man of real flesh and blood, who was somehow at work in you and me as we were helping that old man."

Marcus gave thanks to God in his heart. He felt an overwhelming joy, like a river about to overflow its bank, as he listened to Servianus; he wanted to embrace his friend then and there. He had been praying for this moment for years. But he sensed that Servi had something more to say.

"But even after that," the son of Antonius continued, "I still had doubts, and remained quite influenced by the ideas of Valentinus and Marcion—that is, until I spoke with my sister Livia."

"Your sister Livia!" Marcus exclaimed incredulously. "What could she have to do with any of this?"

"I haven't really kept you up to date on her, Marcus; I'm sorry. Her husband from Capua divorced her, leaving her with just enough to live on, and no children which she always wanted to have. She was miserable for a while living with our mother, who had taken a lover. I tried to help her through the whole thing, but she ended up leaving Agrippina, and going to live with a friend whom Claudia recommended."

"Yes," Marcus said, "I remember that she and Claudia were always very close, even after she married Quintus."

"Exactly so," answered Servianus with the precision of an Aristotelian. "But Livia continued to be very depressed, and once she actually tried to commit suicide by taking some poison. She became very ill, but recovered, thank God."

Marcus could only listen in astonished silence, for he realized that he was hearing the story of the one who had condemned his sister.

"After that very low point in her life, Livia actually came to visit me in my house near the Athenaeum. I was shocked since she had never done so before. I was the one who always visited her. As she walked in, I could see a real sense of purpose and determination in her eyes. She was well dressed, her hair was simply groomed—not gaudily, as before—and she got right to the point with me, after giving me a little kiss on the cheek. 'Servi', she said, 'I would like you to explain something to me about Christianity. I understand that you have been studying it.'"

"As you can imagine, Marcus, my eyes lit up at this possibility, so I began to explain to her the main ideas that I had heard from Valentinus: that salvation comes from an emanation of the One, a highly spiritual creature whose name was Jesus; that he freed us from the slavery of matter, which is evil; that he gave us a special gnosis that allows us to know certain secrets . . ."

"Before I could finish speaking, my sister became very angry with me. She stamped her foot on the floor and said, 'No, Servi. . . . I don't want any of those silly Greek theories. I want to know about the *real* Jesus Christ, Junia's god! The one who was really a man, who worked with his hands, who did miracles, and who died on the cross!'

"I was flabbergasted, Marcus. I could barely speak. In one sentence she had destroyed all the mental constructs that I had made with Valentinus's and Marcion's philosophy. And most importantly, I realized that my sister was right in her view of the Christ."

Marcus could only open his eyes wide, and shake his head. He could hardly believe what he had just heard: Livia, an apologist for the true faith! Yet he had always believed in the power of the Holy Spirit working in people's lives, even the most desperate ones, and in the powerful intercession of the saints. Could Junia and Marcia have been praying for her during these many years?

"That is marvelous, Servianus; the whole thing can only come from God. He has deeply touched your sister's mind and heart."

"But you haven't heard the best part yet, Marcus."

"What is that?"

"Livia and I plan to become catechumens together, and will study under the presbyter Eusebius, who used to live with Atticus. If God so wills, we shall be received into the Church, the *true* one, and be baptized in a year."

It was at that point that Marcus could contain himself no longer. He immediately jumped up from the log they were seated upon, and leaped as high as he could. Then he began to dance and laugh, clapping his hands and shouting, "*Euge! Euge!*" (Hurrah, Hurrah!) So many years, so many prayers answered at last. His boyhood friend also jumped from the bench and embraced Marcus, laughing and also doing a kind of dance. A great weight had been lifted from Servianus's mind and heart. Both of them shouted at the top of their lungs, "Alleluia, Alleluia! Give thanks to the God who made heaven and earth!"

Their two horses, tied to nearby trees, were startled by the sudden noise and clamor of the two men, and began to move about and neigh loudly. But to Marcus and Servianus, the horses simply seemed to be joining them in their celebration.

XLVII.

The day after he saw Servianus, Marcus determined to do even more for the Lord Christ at the Athenaeum. He realized that until then he had been too cautious in his approach, owing to the fear that was still in him. But somehow Servianus's conversion had taken away his fear. He recalled how Numer had encouraged him to bring more of his students and colleagues to the Church, and not to hold back. Two phrases from Scripture keep ringing in his mind, which were the Lord's own words: "Take courage, I have overcome the world," and "You are the light of the world . . . so let your light shine before men." [52]

Yet Marcus didn't want to be foolish, even though he was no longer afraid. He reasoned that God wanted to keep him alive as long as possible, so that he could spread the Gospel of the Christ to many more. He would be able to use to advantage his prestige as the foremost expert on Plato at the Athenaeum. Students now were coming from far distant points in the Empire to hear his commentaries, especially on Plato's *Republic* and *Symposium*. He had built an international reputation as a speaker and philosopher, even though he was not Greek.

In past years there had been a lot of gossip about him at the school. Some had openly speculated that he was a Christian, or that at least he had many Christian friends. He also knew that there were many philosophers in Rome who would love to have his position, who would *kill* to have his position. Crescens, the cynic philosopher, had written a lot against Justin's ideas, and had many disciples in Rome; certainly Valentinus and Marcion disliked Marcus as well. He would have to be careful. Didn't the Master, the same one who said "Let your light shine" also say "Be therefore wise as serpents, but guileless as doves"? [53]

[52] Jn 16:33 and Mt 5:13–14.
[53] Mt 10:16.

He thought of those students that he could approach on the subject of Christ . . . those who by their questions and personal lives seemed more open to Christianity. He could then ask them if they were interested in hearing a special series of lectures on Christian beliefs, and their connection with the Platonic dialogues, especially the *Phaedo* and the *Symposium*. He knew he could make a convincing comparison for them between Plato and Christ, without falling into the error of Valentinus. Then he could see which students had a real interest in Christ, and above all, who would be willing to change their lives in order to follow him. With these he could speak more personally, as Dédicus and Numer had spoken with him.

Come, Holy Spirit, give me the courage and the words. It's all for Christ, and for souls, and for his Kingdom.

The first student that he approached was a young man named Hierax, from Iconium in Phrygia. His questions about Plato in class were always very perceptive, and he seemed to be living a clean life, since he was not enslaved to gambling, alcohol, or sex. There were three others like him in another class that Marcus was teaching. When he approached them about inquiry classes into Christianity, they were immediately interested.

So Marcus established a day to begin his classes. At first he held them in a small room at the Athenaeum itself, but as he warmed up to the subject of the Christian Logos, reviewing Philo's platonic commentaries and his Messianic ideas, he thought it better to start having classes in his own house. "The walls of the Athenaeum have eyes and ears," both Titus and Numer had warned him. So he used the room in his small house, which was atrium, kitchen, and dining room all in one. Ten students were coming by that time; Marcus rather enjoyed the close-knit atmosphere of his home since it promoted a real personal dialogue—very similar to the atmosphere of Socrates's own dialogues, he fancied.

"Philo was a great student of Plato," Marcus began teaching them, once they had moved to his home. "He was able to connect many insights of Hebrew Scripture with Greek ideas, especially having to do with Wisdom. But Christians believe that the ultimate Wisdom of God was in the revelation of the Divine Word or Logos. Jesus Christ for his disciples is truly the Redemptive Word of the Father, who became a human being without ceasing to be divine. . . ."

XLVIII.

In the years following Gaius's death, Aurelia had chosen not to remarry. She found herself to be one of the most sought-after widows in the city. Not only was she still quite attractive, but she was wealthy. She had a close circle of friends that she enjoyed, all of them Patricians, and she would occasionally go out with them to dinner parties and plays. But when they tried to introduce her to a widower looking for a wife, she was cordial, but kept her distance.

The real interest in her life, the person who gave her the most satisfaction, was her son. She often invited Marcus to the family home on the Esquiline, or visited him at his small house near the Athenaeum. "You really should get yourself a better place," she told him. "I'll gladly give you the funds. After all, you're one of the best teachers at the Athenaeum, and students from around the Empire come to you to learn about Plato." Marcus would always thank her, but finished by saying that his home was fine enough for his needs.

She was most concerned, as she always had been, about his religion. Years before she had lost her daughter because of her faith in the carpenter from Galilee; she was in constant fear of losing her son also. Marcus was the only person on earth left to her. In her visits she constantly reminded him of the dangers of his path, and invited him to consider other religions. "There are some new mystery cults coming from the East," she said. "Have you looked into them,

Marcus?" At times Marcus would ride with her in the litter, and one day, as they were passing near the Pantheon, which Hadrian had built fifteen years earlier, she took him inside, and pointed to the images of all the gods and goddesses that adorned its cupola. "Have you thought about all of these, my son? Maybe one of them really exists." "Oh, mother," Marcus laughed, "I would trade them all for one good Christian angel!"

At last she realized that she could not sway him from the Christian god, but she could not stop loving him. And Marcus did not stop loving her either. One winter's day, the year after Numer had left for Egypt, she fell sick. Though very busy with his classes, and helping Justin to write his first defense of Christianity to the Emperor, he found time to visit her every day. He arranged with the slave Syphon to bring meals personally to her chamber, and he even prepared some exotic and tasty dishes which he had learned to make in Egypt.

When she felt better, and her birthday was approaching, Marcus prepared a special surprise party for her. He arranged for his three friends Titus, Proclus, and Philius to go to her house for the occasion. She was surprised to see them all, though she had intuited that Marcus was up to something. They brought out a large couch, the one in Junia's room, and took it to Gaius's study, since it was one of the warmest rooms in the house. They then asked Aurelia to be seated on it, as they began their entertainment for her. First Proclus, who was Numer's famous sidekick, introduced one of his "ballads" to the audience, after an elaborate introduction in which he listed his accomplishments as a singer. But when at last he began to sing he was, as usual, quite off key. Aurelia first felt very embarrassed for him, but was determined to clap for him at the end anyhow, out of respect. But then she saw that the whole thing was a joke when her son, who had brought along a flute but couldn't play it, tried to accompany him.

The next performance was more serious. Marcus had asked Titus, who knew all about Roman politics, to check the archives of the Senate for his father's most famous speeches, such as the one convicting Aulius of crimes in Bithynia. Titus delivered dramatic sections of those discourses in oratorical fashion to them all, while at key points in the speech Marcus, Proclus, and Philius would clap and shout *"Euge! Euge! Bene dixisti!* Another Cato!"— just as Gaius's clients used to do in the Senate. Aurelia at first clapped also and enjoyed what she heard, but then, during the third short speech, she began to cry. Marcus was quite surprised, and asked her what the matter was. She did not want to say it out loud, but asked him to come a bit closer to her, as she whispered: "Oh, Marcus, it reminds me of all of your father's speeches that I did not care about. I was too caught up by my parties and games . . ." Then Marcus hugged her and gave her a kiss: "Don't worry, Mother; I'm sure that God knows now that you loved him very much."

Finally it was time for Philius to perform. Though he could not play as well as Numer, he was fairly skilled with the flute and began to play a lively shepherd's song from Umbria, which was very popular in Rome at the time. Aurelia quickly wiped away her tears and was delighted with it, as she clapped her hands and tapped her feet in time with the music. Marcus took the opportunity to ask her for a dance, which his mother immediately accepted with a little cry of joy. Round and round Gaius's austere study they danced, with a step that Junia had taught them both years before, which she had learned from her friend Marcia.

After the celebration was over, when Marcus and his friends had left, Aurelia was convinced that it was the best party she had ever attended; it had made her feel like a young woman again.

XLIX.

Though Marcus was busy at the Athenaeum, he knew that his greatest work was to bring others to Christ. Something inside his soul kept telling him that his time was running out. He would often reflect on Paul's challenge that Christians had to "be making the most of the time," and that "the form of this world was passing away."[54] Some Christians in Rome actually believed that the Christ was to return very soon, and that the world would end at that point, but Marcus simply wanted to spread his saving word to as many persons as he could, with the time that he had. He often recalled the Lord's parable of the Master returning from a long journey, asking an account of the talents he had given to his servants.[55] He realized that he had been given many talents: now he had to make them render. Numer had often told him the same thing.

In the evenings he would visit with Justin, and helped him to write his Apologeticum, the defense of Christianity to Emperor Antoninus. After spending nearly ten years in Rome, and witnessing the persecution of Christian men and women, Justin thought that he had enough material to write a strong letter. He knew that Antoninus was not a violent man himself, but was only following the Roman law against the Christians. Marcus, being a Roman himself, gave him many suggestions for his text. He helped Justin to see that the Emperor would be convinced not so much by theoretical or philosophical points about Christianity, but by the example of Christian men and women in their daily lives. "Be sure to include," Marcus advised, "evidence on how ordinary Christians conduct themselves: they perform their duties well within their rank, as both slaves and freed men."

"I also want to include," the Samarian said, "specific evidence of their clean lives, whether in marriage or in continence. They have stable families, they are raising their

[54] See Eph 5:15 and 1 Cor 7:31; RSV–CE.
[55] Cf. Mt 25:14-30.

children in peace and good order, and they are not trouble-makers. Really, they have benefited Rome and the entire Empire. But the gods of the non-Christians are really nothing but demons, and at their festivals many crimes are committed."

"Antoninus and his friends might feel insulted by that last point," Marcus suggested.

But the fiery Palestinian answered: "I don't care. Let them see the truth. Perhaps God will change their hearts."

L.

After Justin had sent his long Apologeticum to the Emperor, Marcus kept thinking of other projects that he could undertake for Christ. He had a long list of people that he was praying for—including persons from years earlier in his life. Without his realizing it, his reputation as a man of prayer was being spread. He found that other Christians would actually stop him on the street, and give him intentions to pray for. He thought this was quite unusual, given all of his weaknesses, but he gladly accepted them, both from men and women. He included them in his daily prayers and sacrifices, but especially at the Eucharist.

It also occurred to him—he attributed this to the Holy Spirit—that he could win many graces for people by offering his work for them. Some of it was exciting (he had always enjoyed debating), but a good deal of it was tedious, particularly the long hours that he had to spend reviewing pages of Greek manuscripts to prepare his classes. He thought this was a good imitation of the Master's life, who spent thirty years of his life doing routine labor. Though Marcus did intellectual work, he felt that Christ would accept his effort if he did it for God and others. He knew how many of his Patrician and intellectual friends looked down on manual work, as if it demeaned a man. *If only they knew,* Marcus often thought to himself, *Who it was that chose to do thirty years of manual work in a small village. Perhaps they would change their minds.*

He did not forget Bombolinus, one of his father's most faithful *clientes* (assistants). He had gotten to know him a bit before he left for Alexandria, but he had not seen him again after his father had asked him to leave the house. Through Titus, who knew a lot about political figures in Rome, he found out that Bombo had become a valuable and well-paid assistant to a wealthy quaestor. He and his wife had moved from their old flat to a larger, new house on the Quirinal. Marcus resolved to pay him a visit, hoping that Bombo would remember him favorably.

It was not hard to find the house, since it was the newest mansion on the hill. After he knocked at the door, a tall serving girl who looked to be from Gaul appeared and asked him his business. He introduced himself as an old friend of Bombolinus who would like to see him, and gave her his name. She said that he should have a seat in the front of the atrium. As he waited he prayed for the success of his visit. How he remembered Bombo with his booming voice and aggressive moves: he was always the first to greet his father in the morning, as the political workday began. At times he would annoy Junia and himself with his loud and brash tone of voice—but he had served his father well over the years. Perhaps now he could serve Bombo by introducing him to the faith of Christ.

Within a few minutes the serving girl came back with a serious look on her face. "I'm sorry, sir, but Master Bombolinus does not have time to see you today." Marcus's pride was hurt. "But did you tell him who I was? I've known him for many years, and he used to work for my father. I only need a short time to say hello."

The girl, probably seventeen or eighteen years of age, looked embarrassed and said nothing. Marcus felt that he should not press the issue at that time, and simply shook his head sadly and left.

But the very next day, by coincidence, he happened to see Bombo himself walking down the steps of a courthouse in the new forum. He was giving instructions to a whole group of *clientes*, something that Marcus knew had been the dream of his life. He waited until Bombo had finished speaking, then walked up to him, saying a little prayer to the angels as he always did in uncertain circumstances. He noticed that Bombo had put on quite a bit of weight, and had lost some hair, but his complexion was as ruddy as always, exuding self-confidence.

At first Bombo did not recognize him, so Marcus introduced himself. "Don't you remember me, Bombo? I'm Marcus, son of Gaius Metellus Cimber, who was consul of Rome during the time of Hadrian. You worked for him, and came often to our house on the Esquiline."

The older man at first looked surprised, but then his features hardened and he looked angered.

"And why are you stopping me on the street?"

"Why," Marcus said defensively, "at times we had wine and supper together, when you were working for my father—don't you remember? We used to talk about politics and other things." One of the "other things," Marcus recalled, was precisely about helping Bombo into a preferred position with his father, but he felt it was not appropriate to bring that up.

"Yes, I do remember," the other man said briskly, "but that was before something happened."

"What was that?"

"That was before you became a Christian," Bombo answered, and slowly distanced himself from Marcus, though a little regretfully. He didn't even say goodbye or look back as he walked away.

LI.

Another person that Marcus was praying for was Syphon, his family's slave from Macedonia. His father had purchased him when Marcus was only five years old; though older than himself, Syphon had been a great playmate. Since Gaius was often away at the Senate or on travels, the slave would play hoops with Marcus, or go to the festivals with him, accompanied by other reliable slaves of the house. Marcus grew to love Syphon for his kindness; Gaius and Aurelia valued him for his efficiency. He was a true confidante of them both, and they would often ask his opinion on family or other matters.

When visiting his mother after Gaius's death, Marcus had seen Syphon more, and asked him frequently about his wife and children. He spoke to his mother about granting him his freedom, since he had certainly earned it after so many years of service. But Aurelia was adamant. "He's so valuable to me, Marcus. I can't let him go, since I really couldn't handle the other house slaves without him. And he's absolutely loyal."

"Does he know that I'm a Christian?" her son asked her.

"I'm sure he does, Marcus, and the other house staff do as well. Your father and I never told him, but he's intelligent enough to have guessed it."

Since he had known him for so many years, Marcus thought that he could have more success with Syphon in bringing him to Christ. Surely he would be able to bring up the subject with him now, since he knew that he was a Christian. Perhaps he had some questions that Marcus could answer for him. After visiting with his mother one day after the calends of April, Marcus walked back to the slave quarters, where he had gone for many years to play with Syphon and his children. The older Greek slave was sitting at a small table playing dice with a boy who looked to be about five or six. As soon as Marcus entered, Syphon stood up and bowed, and so did the little one.

"May I help you in any way, Master Marcus?"

"Oh, no, I've just come to say hello, and to speak to you about something. Is that your son?"

"He's actually my grandson, son of Daphne, my oldest girl."

"Yes, I remember her," Marcus said, "very pretty and very smart. Where is she now?"

"She tutors two young women in Greek for a family on the Quirinal Hill. She lives with her husband and children there; her husband's the porter of the house. And how are you, Master Marcus?" he asked politely.

"Oh, Syphon, you can just call me Marcus. I've known you for so many years."

"Oh, no, that wouldn't be right," the slave protested.

Marcus smiled and thought it was a good moment to bring up the subject that he had been praying for. "You know, Syphon, according to my religion it would be all right for you just to call me Marcus, because you and I are truly equal before God. I suppose that by now you have heard that I am a Christian."

"Yes, I know that," Syphon said. "While serving your parents, I heard many of their conversations about you and your sister. It was very painful for them when you also became a Christian, especially for your father."

Syphon's words sunk deep into Marcus's heart; he could feel the old wound inside of him opening again, that is, how much he had disappointed his father by becoming a Christian. It was a wound that perhaps would never heal.

"Yes I know, Syphon, but I have found great meaning and happiness in the Lord Jesus Christ, and I've always prayed that my parents would get to know him also."

"I believe that, sir," answered the slave, with a noble simplicity.

"Have you ever met any Christians besides me?" Marcus asked, hoping that this could spark an interest in him.

"Only a few, Master Marcus. They were very kind people, but they seemed rather unbalanced to me."

"Unbalanced? In what sense?"

"They practice such a dangerous religion, for which they

could be condemned at any time, yet they always seem so joyful, as if they're not afraid to die. In addition they have many children, but what future can they give them? I can't understand them; it seems like madness . . ."

"And do I seem crazy to you, Syphon?"

"No, sir, but I do know that you have caused a lot of pain to your parents. It seems to me that Christianity causes a lot of pain; life is painful enough as it is, Master Marcus."

Marcus remained silent. He knew that for many slaves Christianity was actually a tremendous relief from their pain, since it gave them hope, but he could see that Syphon was not ready to understand that now. He said goodbye to him and patted his little grandson on the head. He would not give up praying for Syphon, just as he would not give up praying for Bombolinus. But it would be a long hard journey. Dealing with his students seemed a lot easier.

That night, as he thought once again of his father, and of Syphon's words about the pain that he had caused him, Marcus could not get to sleep, and began to cry softly.

LII.

The following week Marcus saw Gaius son of Discalus leaving from the urban cohort training ground, and waved to him. Gaius came running across the street, and they greeted each other Roman style. "You must come soon to visit our family, Marcus," Gaius offered him with a winning smile. "We haven't seen you since little Drusilla's birth, and Carmina is now expecting number four!" Marcus agreed right away. Though he spent most of his free time with Titus and Philius and his other friends from the Aventine House, he particularly liked to keep in touch with Carmina's parents Justus and Constantia. He would ride out to their home occasionally to visit with them, since they had a part to play in his sister's conversion years before. He especially liked to speak with Timotheus, who always amazed Marcus with his cheerful and hopeful attitude about things, despite his physical handicap. Marcus gave Timotheus some intentions to pray for, since he knew that he was a "little one" in Christ's eyes, with great power in his prayer. And Timotheus would occasionally give Marcus a gift from his own handiwork, since he was very good at whittling.

But he had not seen Gaius's and Carmina's young family for a long while.

When she heard that Marcus was coming to visit them, Carmina felt privileged, for he was highly admired in the Christian community. His conversion had been a great blessing and encouragement for everyone, being the brother of Junia and the son of Gaius Metellus Cimber, consul of Rome. The story of his being saved on the street by Dédicus was well known, along with the work he was doing at the Athenaeum to bring philosophy students to Christ. In the previous year, ten of them had been baptized. In addition, it was well known to Christians that he had given away all of his father's inheritance to the poor. He made frequent personal visits to those in need, sometimes taking his students from the Athenaeum with him. In addition, though he did not want it to be known, it was rumored that he had been of great help to Justin in writing his Apologeticum for Christians to the Emperor.

And if all that were not enough, the Lord had blessed him with a pleasant and outgoing personality.

For that very reason Carmina knew that she had to be careful when she was near him. Her heart fluttered a bit whenever she saw him, at a Eucharist service or at some family event. Certainly she loved her husband and children very much, but she felt deeply attracted to Marcus . . . perhaps it was his good looks, or his Patrician background, or simply the good-natured way that he laughed. She was happy that he was coming to visit them, but she would have to guard the feelings of her heart toward him. So in a very childlike way she asked the Mother of Jesus, to whom she had always had a great devotion, to assist her.

On the day of his visit, Marcus arrived wearing a clean white toga, with a red cape around his shoulders, since it was close to the ides of January, and therefore quite cold outside. Gaius had a bright fire burning at the hearth, and Carmina was preparing some stewed chicken at the stove. Little Discalus, who was now a hearty boy of six, ran up and gave Marcus a hug, while Drusilla, more reserved, smiled at him shyly from behind her mother's apron. Carmina's mother-in-law Silvia was taking care of little Justus, who had now reached the toddler stage. Carmina, looking very pretty and filled with life in her pregnancy, smiled timidly at Marcus. She could feel her heart flutter as she said, "Welcome, Marcus, we're delighted to have you."

"The pleasure is mine, Carmina. I hope everyone is well," Marcus answered with a little prayer to her angel, and thinking how fortunate Gaius was to have such a lovely young wife.

As the afternoon drew on, little Drusilla and Justus lost their shyness, and wanted to climb onto Marcus's lap. He gave them each a kiss, then showed them a trick with coins that Proclus had taught him. He could make a denarius appear from behind his ears and the children's ears, even though his hands appeared completely empty. They were totally mystified, and laughed with delight. Then he told them some little jokes about people and animals, followed by a scary story about Hannibal, which he ended by saying in a loud and threatening voice, "*Hannibal ad portas!*" [56] When they heard that phrase, all the children, including Discalus, shrieked out with fear, while laughing at the same time.

---

[56] Hannibal was the Carthaginian general who inflicted many severe defeats on the Roman army in Italy during the third century B.C. Roman parents, in order to entertain or frighten their children, used to say "*Hannibal ad portas!*"— meaning "Hannibal is at the gates, so you'd better be good!"

"Now, where did you get all of those children's stories, Marcus?" Gaius asked him teasingly. "Is that what you teach at the Athenaeum?"

"Oh, no," Marcus joked back, "they're far too complex for all the sophisticated minds there; they would never understand them."

At that Carmina herself, who was trying to be more reserved with Marcus, laughed out loud and clapped her hands. "Oh, we know, Marcus, that you tell all your jokes in Greek at the Athenaeum."

Marcus then used her little comment to speak about some of his students who were coming for classes on Christianity in his home. One of them was from Ephesus, who had actually met Dédicus there, and another was a young man just introduced to him by Servianus. "I don't know him well yet," Marcus said, "but he seems quite interested in learning about the Christ."

"It's a miracle," Carmina observed, "that Servianus and his sister Livia are now taking instructions with the presbyter Eusebius. Who could have ever predicted it?"

"You can imagine how delighted I am; it was a real gift from the Holy Spirit. I'm sure that Junia and Marcia had something to do with it," he added, as he pointed his hand upward.

"We'll keep praying for them," Carmina said, "and for all the students that you mentioned."

"And I would like to pray for your friends. Whom do you have in mind?"

It was Gaius's turn to speak. "Regarding that, I have marvelous news. The prefect of the Praetorian Guard Quintus—I'm sure you remember him well—has been asking his assistant more and more questions about the Master's teachings. He is delighted by the birth of his son Sergius, and so is his wife Claudia. As he told Séptimus recently, they're attributing it all to the 'Christian god.'"

"I heard something about that, but now I see the complete story. Another grace from the Master, without doubt, and I understand that all of you" (here he bent over and punched little Discalus gently on the cheek), "had a lot to do with it."

Gaius laughed heartily at that, but Carmina blushed.

"What a supper that was . . ." Gaius said, "but—wait a moment. I'm sure my wife has many things to tell us about her friends, also."

At that point Carmina, drawing little Justus to herself, spoke about some of the women she had met while volunteering her time at the Faustinianum. One of them was named Laelia, the wife of a Sicilian merchant, who was also volunteering her time to help the children; she was not a Christian. They had one child, and had moved recently from Sicily after her husband had set up a grain distribution business in Rome. "She has a big heart," Carmina continued, "and loves to help the orphan children. She also has an excellent voice, and loves to sing."

"Oh ho!" Marcus said teasingly, "now we know why you like her so much!"

Gaius laughed at that, but Carmina smiled self-consciously. "Oh, yes, Marcus," she said. "Please pray for her; I think that someday she can come to Christ."

At that point little Discalus, who had been sitting quietly on his small stool in the corner, walked straight up to Marcus and said: "Master Marcus, can you beat my father in wrestling?"

"Whoa! I don't even want to try!"

"But I heard," answered the six-year-old resolutely, "that you can beat anyone in a wrestling match—even Hercules!"

Marcus laughed loudly at that, but then told the boy more seriously, "I don't know, Discalus, your father is very strong. I'm sure he could beat me in a sword fight, but in wrestling . . ."

At that point Gaius cut them both off.

"Son, I'm sure that Marcus could beat me, but this is not the time to bring that up. Marcus is our guest."

As he could see the lad's disappointment, Marcus came up with an idea.

"Listen, Discalus, I won't wrestle with your father, but I will show you some good wrestling tricks, if you can bring me a couple of blankets."

The boy eagerly asked his step-grandmother Silvia for a couple of blankets which Marcus carefully put on the floor. Then in front of everyone he gave a few lessons to Discalus about how to throw someone to the ground, how to pin a person's arms behind his back, and how to know the other person's moves by looking at his feet. Everyone clapped as Marcus showed little Discalus the key moves, without ever hurting him, but just playing with him. To encourage the boy, he even let Discalus pin him to the ground a couple of times.

But it was getting late.

"I've got to prepare a debate tomorrow, and I have seventy-five pages to read. My oil lamp is waiting up for me. I had better leave now; but I thank you all for the wonderful afternoon." Then the whole family knelt down with him together, facing the East, and prayed to the Lord Christ for those who were sick, for those coming closer to the Faith, and for Pope Pius and his presbyters. At the end of the prayer, Discalus added with the honesty of a child: "And please, God, don't let them kill us anymore."

After Marcus left, the boy went up to his father and gave him a big hug. "Father, do you know what I want to be when I grow up?"

"A centurion? A legionary? The prefect of the Praetorian Guard?"

"Oh, no," the little fellow said decisively. "Even better than that. I want to be like Marcus!"

BETRAYAL

LIII.

Marcus knew that many people wanted his job at the Athenaeum. There were visiting philosophers from Alexandria, Ephesus, and Antioch always arriving in Rome, and looking for employment. Some became private tutors for sons of wealthy families; others began schools of their own, as Justin and Valentinus had done. But the Athenaeum had the great advantage of being a public institution—open to all and at the crossroads of society—where one could really propagate his ideas, and make a name for himself.

He had been very successful, not only with his lectures on Plato at the Athenaeum, but with the private classes in his home. He had brought many to Christ already, and several young men had become catechumens. At times he referred some of his brightest students to Justin, though he had some reservations about Justin's teachings. When one of his students, named Hierax, was about to go to Justin's school, Marcus had a little conversation with him about it. "Justin has tremendous insights, especially about the Logos *spermatikos*,[57] and how all the best insights of the philosophers really lead to the Word Himself, but at times I'm troubled by a certain ambiguity in his speech. At times he presents the Logos as somehow inferior to God, more like Plato's demiurge. I once brought this up with him, but he didn't understand what I was saying."

---

[57] Justin's concept of the Logos *spermatikos* was that the truth about the Word of God and salvation was present in an unformed way, like a seed (Greek *sperma*), in the greatest philosophers before Christ. The revelation of Christ the Logos really brought to fruition their insights and aspirations.

"I'll take that into account. Certainly from the writings of John and Paul we see that the Word is divine," Hierax observed.

"Yes, but the Church's teachers really do not yet have the words to describe the union of Father and Son, or how the Son can unite both the divine and the human in himself. I can understand Justin's dilemma," Marcus said frankly. "I have a feeling that eventually we shall have the right words, which will be unambiguous, but I'm afraid that until that time there will be many heresies and battles.[58] Look at all the harm that Valentinus and Marcion have done here with their ideas."

Besides Hierax, Marcus had eight others coming to see him at that time, and he spoke to them openly about the Christ, as equal to the Father and the Redeemer of all mankind. He loved Paul's statement about Christ, that he was "before all creatures, and in him all things hold together,"[59] and would quote it often, trying to come up with the clearest words that he could to penetrate the mystery.

As he told Gaius and Carmina, he had accepted one student that he did not know very well. Servianus, who was soon to be baptized with his sister Livia, recommended him; he was one of his most intelligent students, and had expressed an interest in learning about the Christ. He was a Roman citizen, a tall man named Sobornus from a town near Puteoli; he had a ready smile for everyone, but never could look Marcus in the eye while speaking to him. Marcus was at first doubtful about him, but he felt that he could not deny Servianus anything, since to his immense joy he and his sister were about to enter the Church. So he accepted him into his home and his private classes about Christianity.

---

[58] At the Council of Nicea (A.D. 325) the Church defined that the Son was truly consubstantial (*omoousios*) with the Father, though many objections would follow.

[59] See Col 1:17.

In one particular session, toward the end of March, Marcus felt moved to speak about Christ more openly. He knew that he was taking a chance, since only one of his students had been baptized. But they seemed very open, even desirous, of hearing something more personal from him, his own convictions on the matter. He had spoken with almost all of them personally, and was confident of their loyalty. Because of his joy over Servianus's conversion, he put away his doubts about Sobornus, and clearly spoke of his personal belief in Jesus Christ to everyone in the room; he also affirmed that the Catholic Church, His Body, was the only way to salvation. He greatly desired to contrast the tenets of Christianity with pagan beliefs, much as Justin had done. The students had very good questions, and most of them seemed to leave quite satisfied with Marcus's answers. But Sobornus was strangely silent and serious during the entire class. It seemed to Marcus that he limited himself to simply writing down every word that Marcus had said on his wax tablet.

"Do you have any questions or objections?" Marcus asked him at the end. "I've noticed that you've taken down my statements, word for word."

"That is what I wished to do, sir; your statements are of great interest to me."

"Do you feel drawn to the Christian religion?" Marcus asked him, with some anxiety in his voice.

The young man smiled at that, a little faintly.

"In a way," he answered.

LIV.

During the next two weeks, Marcus had the distinct impression that he was being watched, though he could not say for sure. Even at the Mass, as he was leaving Marius's house, it seemed to him that someone was following him. He asked

Philius, who had prayed at the same Eucharist and was walking with him to bring food to a poor family, if he thought someone was stalking them. Philius only laughed and said "My dear Marcus, Rome has been filled with people for the last three hundred years who are spying on one another, ever since the time of the Gracchi." [60]

A few days after that conversation, just at sunset, Marcus was working at the desk in his all-purpose room. He was reviewing one of Plato's writings and comparing it with a commentary by Philo which he had just received from Numer in Alexandria. As he was trying to translate one particularly abstruse text from Greek to Latin, he heard three strong knocks at his door. He rose and opened the door, and, to his surprise, there were three fully armed Roman soldiers looking at him, with broad swords at their side. The first soldier had a small papyrus scroll in his hand, and asked him curtly: "Are you Marcus Metellus Cimber, teacher of philosophy at the Athenaeum, and son of Gaius Metellus Cimber?"

"I am," Marcus answered. "What is all this about?"

"I have a warrant for your immediate arrest," the soldier said briskly, a middle-sized man with a slight scar on his right cheek. "You have been accused of being a member of the criminal sect called Christians, and of propagating their subversive ideas, contrary to the law of Rome."

All three soldiers then entered the room, and one of them did an immediate search of his books and personal belongings. The other two stood next to Marcus, guarding him. Though Marcus did not have many things, the soldier found a copy of the Gospel of Luke, and two of Paul's letters, one of which was addressed to the Romans. He also found a small wooden anchor and a cross that Timotheus had made, and which had helped Marcus many times to

---

[60] The Grachii were two brothers (Tiberius and Gaius) who attempted financial and agrarian reforms in Rome for plebeians. They were assassinated by Patrician conspirators around 125 B.C.

pray. The investigating soldier then called one of his companions to look at something in the room, and as the other soldier moved away, Marcus thought it could be a good moment to escape. He could throw the soldier nearest to him to the floor, then rush out the half-open door. But that soldier, perhaps noting Marcus's eyes and movement, promptly returned to the door, closed it, and drew his sword. The other two then promptly joined him, noticing his move. Marcus saw that it was useless. After putting the Christian writings into a leather bag, along with the wooden cross and anchor, they handcuffed Marcus and led him out of the house.

LV.

Marcus's trial was to be held in the same place as Titus's, at the old courtroom on the Capitoline near the Temple of Jupiter. Titus desperately tried to find the same attorney who had defended him, but to no avail, which convinced him that he really had been an angel. But he did find one of the best attorneys in Rome, though he was not a Christian. He had strong argumentative skills and knew the law with great detail. Lucullus was appointed judge, which gave Marcus and Titus some hope, since he had been the one who acquitted Titus before.

Once again, as so many times in the past, the whole Christian community was praying for one of their own, and offered continual prayers and sacrifices for Marcus. He was known and loved by many of them, especially by the poor families that he had helped. His closest friends like Titus, Philius, and Proclus spent long hours in extra prayer, along with fasts. Justus and Consti, Gaius and Carmina organized prayer vigils with other families for him, begging God to save his life. They begged him for a miracle, in the same way as those first Christians in Jerusalem had prayed fervently for the lives of Peter and the other apostles, when they were imprisoned by Herod. [61]

When the trial began, Titus and Proclus were there, watching and hearing everything. They prayed continuously for Marcus, but the evidence against him seemed overwhelming. All the witnesses were Roman citizens. The most direct evidence came from Sobornus, who presented verbatim notes of Marcus's classes, in which the accused had clearly stated that Jesus Christ was the Redeemer and Savior of all mankind, and that it was wrong to offer sacrifices to false gods, including the Roman Emperor. Some of Marcus's other students were also questioned, and although unwilling to hurt Marcus their teacher in any way, they were forced under oath to agree with Sobornus's notes. The other two witnesses testified that they had seen Marcus participate at a Christian service in the house of Marius—and that he had not only prayed Christian prayers, but had gone to receive the body and blood of the Christian god, which they called the Eucharist. Marcus recognized their faces; he wondered how they could have been allowed to enter Marius's atrium, where the Mass was said, and how they could have stayed at the Eucharist beyond the reading of the word, if they were not true Christians.

This time, Marcus reflected calmly, there was no brilliant angel to speak up for him, though he kept praying for one to appear. The evidence was clear, and so was Roman law. Lucullus, scrupulously honest, declared that Marcus was guilty of a capital crime against the Emperor by being a Christian, and therefore had either to renounce his superstition publicly, or face the penalty of death. When after two days Marcus was asked officially whether he would renounce his belief, and offer wine and incense to the Roman gods, he answered in these words: *I refuse to deny my belief in Christ the Son of God, and I refuse to offer homage to the gods and*

[61] See Acts 4:23–31.

goddesses of Rome, who are mere illusions of the imagination, if not actual demons.

The sentence was then given and confirmed: Marcus was to undergo death by beheading at a place to be determined in two weeks from that day, at sunrise.

LVI.

When Aurelia heard of her son's arrest and trial, she was deeply saddened, but not shocked. For years she had known that Marcus was violating Roman law, and that eventually it would catch up with him. Her husband had told her that many times, though she had continued to hope against hope. Now she forced herself to accept the whole event as the will of the gods. He had broken the law of Rome, and faced the ultimate penalty. When the death sentence was given, she did not break down or weep uncontrollably. But she found, to her own surprise, that she was rather calm about it; perhaps, she reflected, it was the effect of her Stoic husband's philosophy upon her over the years.

But she could not stifle the great love she felt for her son, which had been growing steadily since he had returned to Rome from Egypt ten years before. They had been wonderful years for her, especially the last five, as Marcus had tried to console her after the loss of Gaius. With the courage that motherhood gives, she determined to request a personal audience with the Emperor himself on behalf of her son. As the wife of Gaius, his most favored counselor, she had already met Antoninus on several occasions, and had pleased him with her beauty and graciousness. Her bold plan worked: the Emperor granted her an audience on the day after Marcus had been sentenced, which was the calends of April.

Syphon and two other most trusted slaves drove her in the *raeda* to the imperial villa in Lorium, and there, before Emperor Antoninus Pius she begged for the life of her son in these words, which Titus had helped her to compose: "Not only do I ask for his life because of his father, who has done such service to Rome as senator, consul, and personal advisor to yourself, mighty Caesar, . . . but also for my son's own merits: despite his perverse superstition, he has brought great prestige to the Athenaeum, and has drawn many students to Rome from other cities of the Empire to study Plato, thereby increasing the glory of Rome in the field of philosophy. For both of these reasons, I humbly ask that he be exiled rather than executed."

The Emperor was moved by her request and asked her to stay at his villa for another day, so that he could consult with his closest advisors. Aurelia prayed to all the gods and goddesses that she knew during that day, and made a special vow to Minerva, daughter of Jupiter and goddess of wisdom, asking for her son's life. Toward the sixth hour of the following day, however, she was told by an imperial page that Marcus would be given no exception to the law of the Roman Republic. This would amount to favoritism. He had been given a fair trial, and was adjudicated by one of the most honest and competent judges in the city. The sentence therefore must remain.

When she heard the message, Aurelia again remained calm. She knew that she had taken a gamble, but she would not give up. She realized at that point that she would not be granted another audience with the Emperor, but if she wrote him a personal note, it would surely come to his attention. Before returning to Rome she asked for a papyrus scroll and ink quill, and in her best hand she wrote these words:

Most Esteemed Emperor Caesar: thank you for giving me an audience and hearing my petition. I understand and accept Roman law, as my husband always did, and who worked courageously within it for the good of many citizens. I understand and accept that Marcus's death sentence cannot be changed. But I make this personal request, not only as a mother, but as a daughter of an honored Patrician family: that my son not be led through the streets of the city to his punishment, as my daughter was; and that his death be swift and not done in a public place, which would open him to the abuse and cruelty of the mobs.

Junia's death had deeply grieved and humiliated her. Despite hers and Gaius's request, their lovely daughter had been drawn through the streets in a chariot, while many people were calling her "whore" and "traitor." She had been stripped and beheaded before crowds of men shouting obscenities at her in the Colosseum. Aurelia had tried to repress that terrible memory from her mind for a long time, but she could never forget it. Nor could her husband. She did not want her son to suffer the same thing.

On the way back to Rome, as she sat alone in the *raeda* driven by Syphon, with two other slaves at his side, she decided to do something that she had never done before. For some reason, which she could not understand and which she fiercely resisted at first, she felt moved to pray to Junia's and Marcus's god. "Lord Jesus Christ," she forced herself to say out loud, "if you exist and are truly powerful, I beg you to let my son die with dignity; he has served you well." The next day, by personal courier, the Emperor sent her the following answer to her note: that Marcus would not be led through the streets or put to death in the Colosseum or other public place; that he would receive his punishment in the courtyard behind the building where he had been tried; that he would be given good prison quarters, and finally, that he would be allowed to have three visitors before his execution, besides his mother, but they must not be Christians.

LVII.

Those of the Way in Rome, especially Justin and his students, kept praying for their brother in prison. Many of the young men with Justin owed their discovery of Christ to Marcus, and were very disappointed to hear that only non-Christians would be able to visit him. But they kept up their prayers for a miracle.

Since Marcus had visited them a short time earlier, Gaius, Carmina, and their children were particularly affected by the sentencing. The whole family prayed far into the night for Marcus when they heard of it, including little Discalus and Drusilla, who were old enough to understand what was happening. The two children knelt praying to God as long as they could, facing Jerusalem, but finally their small bodies collapsed sleepily into the arms of their parents, who were kneeling with them.

But Gaius was determined to do something more for Marcus. Through his friends in the urban cohort, he was able to discover exactly where Marcus was being held, and through his friend Varistus and Séptimus of the Praetorian Guard, he was able to get himself assigned to be one of the ten soldiers guarding Marcus. His friend was overjoyed to see him, though he could say nothing, not wishing to endanger Gaius's life or reputation.

With the other soldiers present, Gaius was not able to find the time to speak with Marcus: the guards were forbidden to speak with the prisoner except for simple orders or requests. But on the second day of duty Gaius was able to obtain permission to speak with the prisoner for ten minutes privately, through a letter signed by Quintus, Head of the Praetorian Guard. Marcus was amazed that Gaius had been able to see him, though he knew nothing of Quintus's letter.

"I don't have long to speak, Marcus," his friend told him after they had embraced and wished each other the peace of Christ. "Tell me," he said urgently, "do you want to escape? Of the ten guards on duty, I have two who are good friends. I'm convinced that with them I can find a way to overpower the other guards, and bring you to freedom. Through Séptimus, I can arrange to have a fast chariot and horses ready to take you from Rome. You could either go north toward the open country of Umbria, or to Ostia, where we could try to arrange for a ship . . ."

But Marcus interrupted him, shaking his head resolutely.

"Thank you, my brother, but I don't think that God wants that now: my time has come to give him glory. I should not run away. Besides, it would be very dangerous for you and your friends to try to overpower the other guards; I'm sure that there would be bloodshed. You yourself might be killed."

"Yes, but I'm willing to take that risk."

"I thank you for that, Gaius," Marcus said as he grasped his hand. "But the most important thing to consider is your dear family: you have a lovely wife and three children, and one on the way! You should not expose yourself to such danger for my sake."

"I talked with Carmina, and she is praying about the whole thing. She was troubled by my plan, but did not say no . . ."

"What a wonderful wife you have! No, I am sure that God does not want you to take this risk for me. But there is one thing you could do for me, one thing that I desire with all of my soul."

"What is that, Marcus? I'll do anything within my power."

"Could you use your connections with the guards to bring in a presbyter for me? I desire greatly to confess my sins, and to receive the Master's Body and Blood. It has been now almost two weeks. Right now, that is the thing that matters most to me."

"It shall be done, Marcus," Gaius said.

Then he gave his philosopher friend a couple of items that Timotheus had especially made for him: a beautifully whittled anchor, and a cross, both made of olive wood, just like the ones the guards had confiscated in his home. Marcus clasped them both to his chest, as if they were the greatest treasures in the world. That same night, in the very early morning hours, Marcus heard a faint knocking at his door, and a bolt being unlatched. It was Gaius accompanied by Father Eusebius. The presbyter heard his confession, and gave him the Lord's Body and Blood from a tiny package that he carried under his cape.

LVIII.

There were only seven days left until his execution. His mother visited him every day of his imprisonment, and insisted on bringing him his morning and afternoon meals, which she herself had prepared at the mansion on the Esquiline. She kept asking him if he was comfortable, and if he was sleeping normally. For the first two days, she kept speaking to him about small things, like new decorations for the house, some friends that she had seen, and her plans for travel. But Marcus was interested in more personal things; he asked her questions about her family and childhood that he had forgotten or never known, and how she and Gaius had met. She in turn asked him about his classes at the Athenaeum, and his experiences in Egypt. But finally, just four days before his execution date, Aurelia broke down.

"Oh, Marcus," she cried out miserably, "I can't keep up this pantomime anymore. Please have pity on me. You are all that I have left in this life. Junia is gone, my husband is gone; all I have is a large house filled with slaves. My only future is to have parties, to travel, and to hear people say 'I'm sorry' whenever they ask me about my husband or children! Oh, Marcus, you and your love are the only reason for me to stay alive . . . "

"No!" Marcus raised his voice, filled with emotion at his mother's pain. "Don't say that. You have many friends. You have many opportunities. I'm sure that you can find a good man to marry, and end your days in happiness."

"Marcus, don't you understand?" she said almost desperately, as tears began to form in her eyes. "*You* are the only one that I live for. *You* are the one that I love. Everything will be so empty for me now; *you* have been my reason for living during these last five years. If you should die," and here her voice began to waver, "I think I would take my own . . ."

Marcus immediately rose from his chair and put his hand over his mother's mouth. "No, no, mother, don't say those awful words. God is good. He loves you, he will protect you. And even though I know you don't believe in him, I'll ask my God Jesus Christ to send you his grace and consolation. You will find peace and you will not be left alone."

"Oh, Marcus," Aurelia whispered as she impulsively turned away from him, "I must leave now, before I collapse in pain. Yes, please pray for me to your god, please pray for me. I must not see you anymore." Then she immediately left the room, sobbing uncontrollably.

Marcus once again was left tormented in spirit, as he had often been before; would his faith in Christ be the cause of his mother's death? Had it been the cause of his father's death? The accusing awful thought made him tremble, and he begged Christ to have mercy on him. He knew that now his faith in Christ had to go very deep, perhaps deeper than ever before in his life. But he felt absolutely powerless, with his mind completely darkened. No philosophy class or theory could save him now. "For you, O God, are my strength; for you, O God, are my consolation," he said slowly. Then, after a few moments, the brave words of the Apostle came to his mind: "For those who love God, all things work together unto good."[62] He kept praying that passage once and again: they were the words that Father Eusebius had asked him to keep repeating after he gave him Holy Communion—until the end.

[62] Rom 8: 28.

Yes, Christ is the Good Shepherd, Marcus thought, *and he loves my mother more than I do*. She is best in his hands. That gave him some peace, though he was still bothered by doubts and fears, and could not sleep well.

THREE LAST DAYS

LIX.

There were only three days left for his execution, and Marcus had so far received no visitors, except for his mother, Gaius, and the priest. In a way he was happy about this. Now he could prepare himself better for death. He would have more time to think and pray. The person he wanted most to see was Numer, but he knew that at this point it was impossible, not only because Numer was a Christian, but because he was far away in Egypt. Perhaps his friend had just heard about his situation from a Christian traveler from Rome—Philius had written to him as soon as Marcus was arrested—but he would obviously not have time to board a ship, and reach Rome to see him.

Just after sunrise on the second day before his execution, he heard the guards outside the door come to a quick attention, and draw their swords from their scabbards. At first he thought that Gaius and the others were going to try to free him, but then he heard the distinctive sound of a Roman military salute, with voices in cadence and hands touching armor. It must be some high-ranking commander, Marcus surmised, but who could it be? Has there been some change of orders concerning him? Was he to die earlier, or be released?

Within a minute the bolt was loosened, and the door opened widely. It was Quintus, prefect of the Praetorian Guard, in full military uniform.

Marcus was overwhelmed. It had been years since he had spoken to Quintus, when he had been courting Junia, his sister. He had seen him occasionally marching through the streets at the head of the Guard, but Marcus had not spoken with him. He was now a man in his early forties with dark eyes, a strong handsome face with a little scar on his left cheek, and a thick growth of dark hair. Athletic in build, as he always had been, he walked up to Marcus resolutely and extended his arms in greeting. Marcus smiled and immediately grasped his right arm.

"Quintus," Marcus exclaimed. "What brings you here? This is amazing to me."

The son of Cassianus smiled faintly. "Didn't Gaius tell you how he was able to come and see you, and how he was able to bring you the Christian priest?"

It was then, in a moment, that Marcus saw it all. It was Quintus himself who had given Gaius that permission. Only he would have the authority to do it.

"I can only thank you, Quintus," said Marcus, laughing a bit and shaking his head ironically, "I'm astonished. At one point we were not on very good terms."

"Yes," Quintus said, as he sat down on a wooden bench near the open courtyard, where two guards stood at the other side, "I do remember our heated conversation at your family's villa on that August day, when you and I were opposed. You were convinced that philosophy had made Rome great, and I claimed that it was her army."

"Then my sister broke in, remember?" Marcus chuckled at the recollection. "She brought her lyre to the room, and sang a little piece about how music calms the soul."

"Yes," the Praetorian said with a certain melancholy, "that was one of the moments that made me fall in love with her."

"It must have been hard for you. I did put in a good word for you to my sister. I even tried to convince her to renounce her faith in Christ, so that she could save her life, and then marry you."

"I never knew that, Marcus and I thank you for trying," the commander said, as he rose slowly from the bench. "Yes, at first it was very hard for me. But then, as time passed and

I thought more about Junia, I realized that she had embraced a greater love, much stronger than I could give her."

Marcus remained silent. It seemed to him that Quintus was opening a treasure to him, something very intimate and personal; he could only listen. But since Quintus said nothing more, Marcus asked in a low voice. "And what was that greater love?"

"It was the love for her Christian god Jesus. I always had the impression, as we spoke and drew close to one another, that her heart was set on something else, or *someone else*. But she agreed to marry me, because her father wanted her to marry, and she was a very obedient girl."

"You were the best choice of all," Marcus reassured him.

"Thanks for saying that, but I know that in her mind she had made a better choice. Your Christian god is very powerful, Marcus. He not only captured Junia's heart, but I sincerely believe that he changed my wife's attitude about having a family. Because of that I have a strong and healthy son, and another child on the way. I am very grateful to your god, and to the family of Gaius and Carmina."

"Perhaps then," Marcus added with a clever smile, "we were both wrong in our argument on that summer day. I'd like to propose that the question is not which thing has made Rome great, whether the army or philosophy. The question is what *will* make her great."

"I think I know where you're going with that, Marcus. Let me say that I have a strong admiration for you and for all Christians. You have great courage. If a man fights and dies for the Empire, he's considered to be a hero, and will receive special homage. But you Christians, both men and women, are willing to endure incredible pain and die for something greater, with no reward or praise."

"Has it ever crossed your mind, Quintus . . ." Marcus's voice faltered a bit, but then he said it directly: "Have you ever considered becoming a Christian?"

"I've thought of it many times. My assistant Séptimus has

actually invited me to meet one of your presbyters, but I'm not ready for that yet. Being a Christian is more dangerous than facing a thousand Parthian archers, without armor."

Marcus laughed at that, but Quintus remained quite solemn looking, as if he were struggling with something very deep inside of him. After they said goodbye, Quintus stepped outside; all the guards immediately came to attention and saluted him, but Junia's brother kept saying a prayer to the Holy Spirit for his conversion.

LX.

The next day, again just after sunrise, there was a knock at his door, and the bolt was loosened. His second visitor was not an adult, but a boy of eleven years old, with dark eyes and hair. There was something familiar in his face, but Marcus could not place him.

"Don't you remember me, Master Marcus?" the lad said, noticing his perplexed look. "I'm Lucius, the boy that you saved from the murderous *raeda* three years ago during the Saturnalia."

"Yes, now I remember," Marcus replied with a warm smile, as he walked over to him. "You've grown taller since then. How are you? Where are your parents?"

"My father is outside with the soldiers. When I heard that you were arrested, I told my parents that it was my greatest desire to see you. After all, you saved my life. Right away my father went to the courthouse and asked permission to visit you; we received it in two days. Now," the boy added with a clever grin on his face, "now I know that you are a Christian."

"Yes," Marcus joked, "I would be a pretty stupid fellow if I weren't one."

The boy laughed, and extended his hand for Marcus to shake it.

"Well, I'm grateful that you came to visit me, Lucius.

I'm afraid that I can't invite you for a hike, or a horseback ride."

"That's all right. I just wanted to see you and thank you once again for what you did for me that night. I am very sorry that you will have to die."

"We must all die someday, Lucius. But you should realize that you also helped me that night of the Saturnalia, in a way that only God and I know. Do you know that once in my life a man also saved me from being run over by a chariot, in the middle of the street?"

The boy opened his eyes widely, and whistled through his teeth in wonder.

"Was he a Christian also?"

"He was learning to become one at that time."

"And did he become one in the end?"

"Yes."

At that the boy became quite serious, as if he were thinking of something important. He didn't say anything for a while, and began to shuffle his feet a little bit, so Marcus asked him what he was thinking.

"Master Marcus, I think that I would like to become a Christian someday, so that I can be just like you and your friend."

Then he asked Marcus if he could give him a final hug, and was escorted out of the room by the guards to his father.

LXI.

Marcus thought that he would have no more visitors that day, but at the tenth hour, he heard a knock and the door bolt being loosened again. The door opened, and instead of one person, two individuals entered. It was Servianus with a woman who seemed much older than he, though it was not his mother. After looking at her more closely, he was shocked to see that it was his sister Livia. He had not seen her for more than fifteen years; she should have been in her early thirties, but she looked much older. There were deep lines on her face and forehead, and she looked very tired. Her eyes were red, the sign that she had been crying a lot.

Servianus, filled with emotion on seeing his friend, ran up to Marcus and embraced him, while Livia stood near the door, trembling and uncertain of herself.

"Oh, my friend, my dear friend! Can you ever forgive us and my family for what we have done to you?"

Marcus at that moment could barely speak, "Servi," he said faintly, "it's the Lord Christ who forgives . . . both you and me, and everyone. I hold no anger against you or your family, especially now as I prepare to meet God."

"But, Marcus, please understand my feelings. When I recommended Sobornus to attend your classes on Christianity, I had no idea that he was a spy. He seemed to me genuinely interested in learning about the Church, and from what I could see, he was a sincere and honest person."

"I know that, Servi. You intended only to spread the word of Christ to another person, and you thought he was sincere. Remember that among the Lord's first twelve, one was a traitor. I'm sure that there will be treachery within the Church until the end of time. Besides, there were other witnesses against me; Sobornus was not the only one."

"Yes, that thought has consoled me, but it is still very hard for me."

"And yet," they heard a soft feminine voice groaning from the other side of the room, "I have no such consolation. My mother and I were the cause of Junia's death."

Marcus didn't know what to say. The shock of seeing Livia after so many years paralyzed him; he felt so many conflicting emotions that he could say nothing.

At that point the daughter of Antonius and Agrippina approached Marcus, and looked up into his eyes.

"Oh, Marcus, can you ever forgive me? Can your mother ever forgive me for what I have done?"

Marcus at last found his voice, but it was beginning to

crack. "Of course I . . . of course I forgive you, Livia—and the Lord will forgive you. And besides, wasn't it your father and your mother who were behind the whole plot? Weren't they the ones who hired Culebros, and then later tried to spy on me?"

"Yes, yes," Livia answered in an agonized tone of voice, "but it was I who hated her! I couldn't stand Junia's good looks and intelligence . . . she only infuriated me, and then, when Quintus proposed to her, I went insane." After that she turned away to her brother, and began to cry on his chest.

Marcus felt like taking Livia into her arms, and kissing her, and telling her that it would be all right—but something stopped him. Everything was coming too quickly upon him: his whole life, past and present, and the lives of his father, mother, and sister were overwhelming him in an avalanche of memories, both good and bad. He simply dropped to his knees, and made the sign of the cross. He had to ask Christ for help.

Immediately Servianus and his sister dropped to their knees beside him. In the emotion of the moment, Marcus had forgotten that they were both catechumens, and would be baptized very soon at the Easter Vigil. He found that his lips began to move of their own accord, though he knew and felt what he was saying: "O Lord Jesus Christ, I pray to you for Servianus and Livia: please take the pain from their hearts. For it was you who said 'Come to me all you who labor and are heavily burdened, and I will give you rest.' Please give rest to both of them, this brother and sister of mine. Give them a great peace, and bring them to your eternal kingdom someday, where they will be with you and your beautiful Mother forever and ever. Amen."

They all remained kneeling and in silence after that, for about five minutes. Then Marcus stood up, and the other two with him. Both Servianus and Livia were much calmer now. Marcus could see a more relaxed look on their faces, even the beginning of two little smiles.

Servianus was the first to speak. "Very soon, Marcus, in one week, Livia and I will become children of God, and receive the flowing water of his forgiveness and grace. But we had to visit you first, before that happened: we *had* to."

Taking her brother's hand into hers, Livia then added in a calm voice. "It's something that we've been preparing to do for a year, as you know, Marcus. And we have come to believe that through Baptism all our sins will be washed away."

"And you believe truly," Marcus said. "Just as my sins were washed away in the catacomb where Junia is buried, on my day of Baptism. It was the happiest day of my life, and I wish you both the same."

"I've already visited that catacomb ten times," Livia said, now with a certain pride and confidence in her voice. "I've prayed to both of them, to Marcia and Junia, for their forgiveness, and I cried each time I was there. Oh," she said in a quick shift of mood, and with a little laugh, "what a fun sort of girl Marcia was!"

Marcus now really wanted to embrace Livia, something that he had been loathe even to think about for many years; but all of that was falling from him now, like the scabs of an old wound. He felt that his soul was being filled with a new wave of love, which had to be coming from the Master.

There was an abrupt knock at the door. A guard entered and announced that the hour had gone by, and the visitors had to leave. Marcus turned to Servianus and embraced him for the last time, then he turned to Livia and embraced her also, kissing her twice on the forehead.

She looked up at him with something like joy and adventure in her eyes, and he realized in an instant that she was the last woman he would see on earth. "Oh, Marcus," she said, "please tell Junia, when you see her, to keep helping me!"

LXII

It was Marcus's last day. He was grateful to be able to spend it alone, to pray more and prepare his soul for death. He kept giving thanks above all for the three visits he had received, each of them totally unexpected, each a gift from God. Quintus's honesty, Lucius's interest in the Faith, and best of all, Servianus and his sister, who would soon become his brother and sister in Christ. God had comforted him greatly, and given him strength for his final ordeal . . . yet none of his visitors were Christians, according to the Emperor's order. What a marvel!

He walked around his small room again and again, and occasionally into the courtyard, where a light breeze was blowing on the poplar tree next to the fountain, and where two guards stood at the far wall. It was good of his mother to arrange for such a pleasant place for him to be; he could pray more easily now. Yes, his mother . . . she needed his prayers most of all, he was convinced. Now she would feel all alone. *Lord, may she find meaning to her life, may she never harm herself.* On his knees he prayed that somehow, through a miracle of grace and providence, she would discover Christ at last. He prayed for his father, who had died smiling at him, with God's name on his lips; surely Christ would have mercy on him also. He prayed for Justin, Titus, Proclus, Philius, and his closest companions in the city. Like him they had chosen the path of celibacy for Christ, which for them was the pearl of great price. May they never lose it! He prayed for all the families he had known, for those married couples and their children . . . for Justus and Consti, for Gaius and Carmina. They were in just as much danger as he was, for they too could be denounced as Christians by some rival or enemy. But with their children and grandchildren they were building up Christ's body on earth, and spreading his kingdom. He prayed for Timotheus, who was given a special share in the Master's cross:

he could almost feel Timo's prayers bolstering and encouraging him.

But after his mother, the person he remembered the most was Numer. How much he owed to that short, entertaining African who had first spoken to him about complete dedication to Christ. He knew that Numer was praying hard for him, wherever he was. He must have received Philius's letter by now, and probably, at that very moment, he was trying to reach Rome by land or sea in order to see him. But it didn't matter. Numer had already given him a gift that had changed his life: a joyful and adventuresome spirit. It was he who had first spoken to him of the Love of loves, the hundredfold, and he had freely chosen to take the same path. It was Numer who had always insisted that he try to serve Christ right where he was in the city, through his work as a teacher at the Athenaeum. Marcus begged the Lord of the harvest to keep sending to his Church, in the years ahead, many men like him and many women like Marcia; for they both had the gift of being true friends, and of bringing others to Christ in such a natural and encouraging way.

At one point, when he was in the courtyard trying to pray, a large hawk suddenly swept down toward him, right above his head, then turned skyward again. A bad omen? It frightened him for a moment, and reminded him of what was going to happen to him the next day at sunrise. How easy it would be now to give in to those old fears and doubts; how easy it would be to run away from Christ, and worship once again the old Roman gods and goddesses. He could save his life, and keep his position at the Athenaeum, if it was not already taken by the person who hired Sobornus.

"No!" Marcus groaned as he shook his head resolutely, "begone Satan." Then he punched the air, as if trying to hit with his fists the evil one who was tempting him. "The Lord is one, and him alone shall you serve," he said out loud, though he knew that the guards would think that he was crazy. They probably already thought that he was crazy, since he was a Christian.

He had been able to get a small hourglass to keep time. At the third, sixth, and ninth hours of the day he knelt down facing East—while holding the little wooden anchor and cross that Timotheus had given him. He thought of the Master and his sufferings. At the third hour, he was sentenced; at the sixth hour he was crucified; at the ninth hour he died. *Divine Master, may I be faithful to you, until the end! And how fortunate I am, Lord, to have so many praying for me right now,* though he could see and hear nobody . . . only the loud laughs and curses of the guards outside, and the distant clamor of the Roman streets beneath him.

He thought often of Dédicus and Atticus. How much he owed to these his dearest friends, and what a delight to be with them forever. What a joy to see Junia, and give her Livia's message, and then to dance with her, dance *forever*, as she had always wanted, and never grow tired. Marcus laughed as he held the little wooden cross and anchor in his hands, and kissed them.

Poor Junia, who had endured such misunderstanding that last month of her life from himself and from her parents, and such abuse from the crowds shouting obscenities at her. But for him, because of her mother's petition to the Emperor, his confinement had been very peaceful and easy. Junia had cried constantly in her suffering; she had been visited by no one, except Cynthia. Yet six people had visited him, including Gaius and the priest. *O Lord Christ*, Marcus prayed, *give me a bigger taste of your cross. Just as you had, just as my sister had, let me also have mockery and pain, before I die . . .*

For the rest of the day he kept thinking about what heaven would be. Would meeting the Lord be a great intellectual experience? He had been thinking and talking about the Logos for the last twenty years of his life; would Christ therefore appear to him as the final and culminating Idea?

That seemed reasonable since he was a philosopher. Yet somehow he preferred to see Christ simply as the good shepherd, like that strong and smiling young man painted on the catacomb wall above his sister's tomb, and holding a lamb; yes, that is the Christ he wanted to see and love. He dreamed of the Lord's taking him into his strong arms, putting him on his shoulders, and maybe even challenging him to a wrestling match, and he would win! And then, after all that, Christ would sit down and talk about the deepest and most exciting philosophical questions with Dédicus and him, giving them his truth, and forever opening new and marvelous horizons for them.

He didn't sleep that night, though he did lie down on his couch. He kept saying "*Iesu, te amo; Iesu, adiuva matrem meam; Jesu et Maria, ut maneam semper vobiscum.*" [63] At times he would drift off to sleep, but he woke up many times; when that happened, he tried to keep praying.

---

[63] English: "Jesus, I love you; Jesus, help my mother; Jesus and Mary, may I remain always with you."

GRAIN OF WHEAT

LXIII.

Just at sunrise there were three loud knocks on the door, and, once again, he heard the bolt being unlatched. He rose from the couch, and knelt on the floor facing Jerusalem, praying to Christ for strength and calm. He realized that for the next ten minutes he must not only give glory to God, but help the Roman guards to see Jesus' courage in him. Perhaps it could be the beginning of conversion for one or two of them. He followed the soldiers out of the door to the open yard behind the courthouse where he had been tried. He walked behind them with a firm step, and a little expectant smile on his face. Very soon he would be facing Christ. *O Lord, forgive me for my sins, especially those that I committed before I was a Christian . . . but I know that your blood and sacraments have washed them all away.*

They came to the open yard, surrounded by a long stone wall. It was a cloudy day, and there was a cool breeze coming over the wall. At the center of the yard was a dark square wooden block, slightly hollowed out in the center where he was to place his head. He had never seen a block like that before, and once again, he felt afraid; he stopped walking for a moment, and looked around him. Still time to save his life, still time to run from Christ. *No, I won't run, just as Christ did not run: He agonized for hours on the cross, but for me it will be over in an instant. "Iesu Iesu, fortitudo mea et salvator meus,"* [64] he prayed silently, then continued to walk forward with a firm step behind the soldiers.

---

[64] English: "Jesus, Jesus, you are my strength and my Savior."

He was nearly halfway to the execution block between the two rows of guards, when his eye caught sight of a familiar face. One of the guards, he was sure, was the son of a man that his father had once saved from bankruptcy and disgrace. He had met him when he was a teenager, but his face had not changed that much. It was the same person, he was sure; they had become friends during those years, and the boy's family was extremely grateful to his father. Marcus looked at him as he walked by, and despite the absurdity of his situation, he smiled slightly and waved at him. But the man only looked at him coldly, and as Marcus walked by him he heard him say in a low but very distinct voice: "Disgrace! Disgrace to your father!"

For Marcus that comment was like a knife going through his heart, even before the executioner's axe was to strike him. He simply looked away helplessly, and said a prayer for the man. As he approached the wooden block, it occurred to him that God had granted him his petition from the day before. He had asked for insults, and had just received a brutal one in the last moments of his life.

Then slowly, very deliberately he knelt down and laid his head on the hard wooden block. As he began to pronounce slowly the Lord's last words, "Into your hands I commend my spirit," he could hear the soldier stretching his arms above him and lifting the axe. The cool soft breeze was now caressing his face, and there was a moment of total silence. Junia's brother heard the sound of the axe blade falling in a whisk of air above his head, and then, after an instant of indescribable pain, everything became light, a glorious golden Light enfolding him. He knew that he was home at last.

LXIV.

During the week after her son was killed, Aurelia kept walking around the empty rooms of the big mansion on the Esquiline. Each one had such meaning for her: Junia's chamber, with the little table and looking glass, and the mosaic of a white ship sailing on the blue sea; Gaius's study with its large marble desk and matching oak wood chair; their bedroom, where they had shared their love as man and wife so many times; Marcus's room, with the small table in the corner he used for writing, and a bust of Plato in the corner. Though he had not slept there for many years, it was the room that she visited the most.

What had life to give her now? Her whole family was gone. Should she look for a husband at her age? Though she was still attractive, she knew that any man courting her now would only be interested in her money. Should she simply try to forget about everything and give herself to plays and parties, as she had done in the years before Junia died? Or should she spend her whole day looking in the mirror, hiring expensive cosmeticians to arrange her hair, and using exotic perfumes?

So many thoughts came to her mind, but she rejected them one by one. Above all, she kept thinking of Marcus. *Oh, Marcus*, she said to herself aloud, *how much pain I caused you, without wanting to do so!* She and her husband had only thought about the pain that Marcus had caused them by becoming a Christian, but they had never thought of the pain that they were causing *him*. Now she realized it. Her son had been true to the end to his god, the crucified carpenter from Nazareth. Despite all of her tears and threats— even to take her own life—Marcus had remained true to his Faith. He had always been kind to her: not one impatient or angry word in years. *He was a hero, really, and I never recognized it*, she thought to herself. For not only had he become a Christian, at great risk to himself, but he had also given up the right to have a wife and children of his own, for the love of his god, and had lived in celibacy for the rest of his life.

She sat down at his desk, and toyed with the little wooden cross and anchor that they had given her after his beheading; they were the only possessions they found in his room. A cross and an anchor, she reflected. Perhaps the cross is for their Christ who was crucified . . . but the anchor? Could it have to do with the mosaic of the ship that Junia had put in her room? She remembered that she had prayed to Jesus Christ for her son to have a peaceful death, without abuse from the crowds, and as far as she knew, Christ had granted that prayer to her. So why couldn't she pray to Marcus himself now, if at last he was with his god? *Marcus my son*, she said out loud while holding the little cross and anchor in her hands, *wherever you are, please help me. I feel so lonely now . . . there's no meaning in my life anymore.*

The next day Aurelia asked Syphon and three other slaves to prepare her litter to go into the city. She wanted to go by the Athenaeum, where her son had worked for more than ten years, and to visit his small house nearby, though it had already been confiscated by the magistrates of Rome. She felt that by visiting these places she could somehow be closer to him, and perhaps ease her pain. As she was about to leave the atrium, she saw the bronze bowl for burning incense to the image of Minerva that she had placed at the entrance. She had always put a bit of incense there, to honor the goddess, whenever she left the house. But today for some reason she decided not to do it; she felt that something else was about to come into her life, though she had no idea what it could be.

Four servants transported her down the Esquiline Hill to one of the main streets of the city that led to Hadrian's Athenaeum. As they pushed through the crowds, she saw all kinds of people teeming around her: plebeians with soiled togas, freed men and women, visitors from provinces throughout the Empire, and above all slaves, both male and female, of many different sizes and skin colors. Some individuals were walking briskly, with determination; others walked aimlessly, as if they had no idea where they were going; some were talking with a companion; still others walked alone and in silence. It was the third hour, and many of them were going to shops and markets in order to purchase items for the day. She thought of how often Marcus had walked on that very street, among those same people; he had not wanted to take a litter or carriage, and would come home perspiring with the smells of the city on him. She and Junia used to scold him then for being so common, and not acting like a Patrician.

Suddenly she had an idea: she wanted to experience what Marcus had experienced so many times. She asked the slaves to lower the litter, so that she could get out and walk among the people. Syphon, who walked in front of the litter with another slave clearing the way, expressed his amazement and disagreement: he said that he was her loyal servant, that she had never done this before, that she could be hurt. But Aurelia insisted, and he had to obey. She stepped from the litter. Syphon and two of the other slaves offered to go with her, but she refused. "I want to walk in the street alone, as my son did," she said. She was wearing a light purple cape over her long tunic, with no jewelry or special makeup . . . so she thought she would not attract much attention to herself. She would be just one more woman in the crowd, not a Patrician lady. She passed by a man who had practically no teeth and very bad breath, and another who was half-drunk. A couple of off-duty soldiers were telling jokes, and one of them made an obscene sign at her. One plebeian woman, dressed in a dark brown tunic, almost ran her down; she seemed to be in a great hurry to get somewhere.

Aurelia began to feel silly and confused for what she was doing, even a little angry at herself. She was about to turn back to the litter, where Syphon was waiting for her, when by chance she caught sight of the familiar face of a woman to her left, walking quickly. It was Cynthia, her daughter's personal servant for many years. Aurelia had not seen her since Gaius had dismissed her from their house, shortly after Junia's death, but she had heard from Marcus that she had become a Christian. For some reason, which she could not understand, she began to run after her and call her name. She could see her through the crowd, about twenty-five feet to her left, walking toward a fish-shop. (Cynthia was actually going to buy food at Discalus's shop for the orphan girls at the Faustinianum, since Discalus always gave her a generous discount.) Pushing people to the side, and running, Aurelia got to within ten feet of her, and called her name again, this time quite out of breath.

"Cynthia, Cynthia," she raised her voice, "don't you remember me?"

The Greek woman, now in her early thirties, was startled, and turned around to see the older blonde-haired woman waving to her. Of course she remembered her: how could she forget her first mistress in Rome, and Junia's mother? She had actually been praying for Aurelia for many years, after becoming a Christian. Scintilla had constantly reminded her to do so. During the last week she had actually been praying more for her because of Marcus's death. But she was amazed now to see Aurelia walking in the street like a plebeian: she had never done that before. And there was an anxious, almost eager look on her face, which she had never seen before.

Finally Aurelia caught up with her, and embraced her. It was the first time in her life that she had ever embraced a slave, or a former slave, but she didn't care.

"Cynthia," the mother of Marcus and Junia said warmly, "how are you? It's been so long. You must come to visit me at my house on the Esquiline. It's so empty now."

"Yes it must be," Cynthia answered, looking at her with amazement. "I was very sorry to hear about Marcus; it must be a great loss for you. It has been for all of us. But what should we talk about if I were to visit you? We have such totally different lives now, Mistress Aurelia." Without thinking about it, in the excitement of the moment, Cynthia had slipped into addressing her as she had done years before, as a slave, when Junia was alive.

"What should we talk about?" Aurelia answered enthusiastically, as if she were a girl of fifteen. "About everything! About where you have been, and what you are doing now. About your friends. About me, and my life. But above all, Cynthia, I want you to tell me about Jesus Christ, and why my children loved him so."

Finis